The Short Stories Of Elizabeth Gaskell

The short story is often viewed as an inferior relation to the Novel. But it is an art in itself. To take a story and distil its essence into fewer pages while keeping character and plot rounded and driven is not an easy task. Many try and many fail.

In this series we look at short stories from many of our most accomplished writers. Miniature masterpieces with a lot to say. In this volume we examine some of the short stories of Elizabeth Gaskell.

Elizabeth Gaskell is equally well known as Mrs Gaskell. When her mother died, she was three months old and she was sent to live in Knutsford, Cheshire with her Aunt Hannah, this setting would become the basis for her novel Cranford. At 22 she married and settled in Manchester to raise her family. Friends with Charlotte Bronte she went on to write her biography and was also highly regarded by a certain Charles Dickens who published her ghost stories in his magazine. Much of her work views the emerging industrial society of Victorian England through her own moral and religious values and has an uncanny ability to look at and report on the many strata of society.

Some of these stories are also available as an audiobook from our sister company Word Of Mouth. Many samples are at our youtube channel http://www.youtube.com/user/PortablePoetry?feature=mhee The full volume can be purchased from iTunes, Amazon and other digital stores. Among the readers are Richard Mitchley, Eve Karpf & Ghizela Rowe

Index Of Stories

The Old Nurse's Story

You know, my dears, that your mother was an orphan, and an only child; and I dare say you have heard that your grandfather was a clergyman up in Westmorland, where I come from. I was just a girl in the village school, when, one day, your grandmother came in to ask the mistress if there was any scholar there who would do for a nurse-maid; and mighty proud I was, I can tell ye, when the mistress called me up, and spoke to my being a good girl at my needle, and a steady honest girl, and one whose parents were very respectable, though they might be poor. I thought I should like nothing better than to serve the pretty young lady, who was blushing as deep as I was, as she spoke of the coming baby, and what I should have to do with it. However, I see you don't care so much for this part of my story, as for what you think is to come, so I'll tell you at once. I was engaged and settled at the parsonage before Miss Rosamond (that was the baby, who is now your mother) was born. To be sure, I had little enough to do with her when she came, for she was never out of her mother's arms, and slept by her all night long; and proud enough was I sometimes when missis trusted her to me. There never was such a baby before or since, though you've all of you been fine enough in your turns; but for sweet, winning ways, you've none of you come up to your mother. She took after her mother, who was a real lady born; a Miss Furnivall, a granddaughter of Lord Furnivall's, in Northumberland. I believe she had neither brother nor sister, and had been brought up in my lord's family till she had married your grandfather, who was just a curate, son to a shopkeeper in Carlisle—but a clever, fine gentleman as ever was—and one who was a right-down hard worker in his parish, which was very wide, and scattered all abroad over the Westmorland Fells. When your mother, little Miss Rosamond, was about four or five years old, both her parents died in a fortnight—one after the other. Ah! that was a sad time. My pretty young mistress and me was looking for another baby, when my master came home from one of his long rides, wet, and tired, and took the fever he died of; and then she never held up her head again, but just lived to see her dead baby, and have it laid on her breast before she sighed away her life. My mistress had asked me, on her death-bed, never to leave Miss Rosamond; but if she had never spoken a word, I would have gone with the little child to the end of the world.

The next thing, and before we had well stilled our sobs, the executors and guardians came to settle the affairs. They were my poor young mistress's own cousin, Lord Furnivall, and Mr. Esthwaite, my master's brother, a shopkeeper in Manchester; not so well-to-do then as he was afterwards, and with a large family rising about him. Well! I don't know if it were their settling, or because of a letter my mistress wrote on her death-bed to her cousin, my lord; but somehow it was settled that Miss Rosamond and me were to go to Furnivall Manor House, in Northumberland, and my lord spoke as if it had been her mother's wish that she should live with his family, and as if he had no objections, for that one or two more or less could make no difference in so grand a household. So, though that was not the way in which I should have wished the coming of my bright and pretty pet to have been looked at—who was like a sunbeam in any family, be it never so grand—I was well pleased that all the folks in the Dale should stare and admire, when they heard I was going to be young lady's maid at my Lord Furnivall's at Furnivall Manor.

But I made a mistake in thinking we were to go and live where my lord did. It turned out that the family had left Furnivall Manor House fifty years or more. I could not hear that my poor young mistress had ever been there, though she had been brought up in the family; and I was sorry for that, for I should have liked Miss Rosamond's youth to have passed where her mother's had been.

My lord's gentleman, from whom I asked as many questions as I durst, said that the Manor House was at the foot of the Cumberland Fells, and a very grand place; that an old Miss Furnivall, a great-aunt of my lord's, lived there, with only a few servants; but that it was a very healthy place, and my lord had thought that it would suit Miss Rosamond very well for a few years, and that her being there might perhaps amuse his old aunt.

I was bidden by my lord to have Miss Rosamond's things ready by a certain day. He was a stern proud man, as they say all the Lords Furnivall were; and he never spoke a word more than was necessary. Folk did say he had loved my young mistress; but that, because she knew that his father would object, she would never listen to him, and married Mr. Esthwaite; but I don't know. He never married at any rate. But he never took much notice of Miss Rosamond; which I thought he might have done if he had cared for her dead mother. He sent his gentleman with us to the Manor House, telling him to join him at Newcastle that same evening; so there was no great length of time for him to make us known to all the strangers before he, too, shook us off; and we were left, two lonely young things (I was not eighteen), in the great old Manor House. It seems like yesterday that we drove there. We had left our own dear parsonage very early, and we had both cried as if our hearts would break, though we were travelling in my lord's carriage, which I thought so much of once. And now it was long past noon on a September day, and we stopped to change horses for the last time at a little smoky town, all full of colliers and miners. Miss Rosamond had fallen asleep, but Mr. Henry told me to waken her, that she might see the park and the Manor House as we drove up. I thought it rather a pity; but I did what he bade me, for fear he should complain of me to my lord. We had left all signs of a town, or even a village, and were then inside the gates of a large wild park—not like the parks here in the south, but with rocks, and the noise of running water, and gnarled thorn-trees, and old oaks, all white and peeled with age.

The road went up about two miles, and then we saw a great and stately house, with many trees close around it, so close that in some places their branches dragged against the walls when the wind blew; and some hung broken down; for no one seemed to take much charge of the place;—to lop the wood, or to keep the moss-covered carriage-way in order. Only in front of the house all was clear. The great oval drive was without a weed; and neither tree nor creeper was allowed to grow over the long, many-windowed front; at both sides of which a wing projected, which were each the ends of other side fronts; for the house, although it was so desolate, was even grander than I expected. Behind it rose the Fells, which seemed unenclosed and bare enough; and on the left hand of the house, as you stood facing it, was a little, old-fashioned flower-garden, as I found out afterwards. A door opened out upon it from the west front; it had been scooped out of the thick dark wood for some old Lady Furnivall; but the branches of the great forest trees had grown and overshadowed it again, and there were very few flowers that would live there at that time.

When we drove up to the great front entrance, and went into the hall I thought we should be lost—it was so large, and vast, and grand. There was a chandelier all of bronze, hung down from the middle of the ceiling; and I had never seen one before, and looked at it all in amaze. Then, at one end of the hall, was a great fire-place, as large as the sides of the houses in my country, with massy andirons and dogs to hold the wood; and by it were heavy old-fashioned sofas. At the opposite end of the hall, to the left as you went in—on the western side—was an organ built into the wall, and so large that it filled up the best part of that end. Beyond it, on the same side, was a door; and opposite, on each side of the fire-place, were also doors leading to the east front; but those I never went through as long as I stayed in the house, so I can't tell you what lay beyond.

The afternoon was closing in, and the hall, which had no fire lighted in it, looked dark and gloomy, but we did not stay there a moment. The old servant, who had opened the door for us, bowed to Mr. Henry, and took us in through the door at the further side of the great organ, and led us through several smaller halls and passages into the west drawing-room, where he said that Miss Furnivall was sitting. Poor little Miss Rosamond held very tight to me, as if she were scared and lost in that great place, and as for myself, I was not much better. The west drawing-room was very cheerful-looking, with a warm fire in it, and plenty of good, comfortable furniture about. Miss Furnivall was an old lady not far from eighty, I should think, but I do not know. She was thin and tall, and had a face as full of fine wrinkles as if they had been drawn all over it with a needle's point. Her eyes were very watchful, to make up, I suppose, for her being so deaf as to be obliged to use a trumpet. Sitting with her, working at the same great piece of tapestry, was Mrs. Stark, her maid and companion, and almost as old as she was. She had lived with Miss Furnivall ever since they both were young, and now she seemed more like a friend than a servant; she looked so cold and grey, and stony, as if she had never loved or cared for any one; and I don't suppose she did care for any one, except her mistress; and, owing to the great deafness of the latter, Mrs. Stark treated her very much as if she were a child. Mr. Henry gave some message from my lord, and then he bowed good-bye to us all—taking no notice of my sweet little Miss Rosamond's outstretched hand—and left us standing there, being looked at by the two old ladies through their spectacles.

I was right glad when they rung for the old footman who had shown us in at first, and told him to take us to our rooms. So we went out of that great drawing-room, and into another sitting-room, and out of that, and then up a great flight of stairs, and along a broad gallery—which was something like a library, having books all down one side, and windows and writing-tables all down the other—till we came to our rooms, which I was not sorry to hear were just over the kitchens; for I began to think I should be lost in that wilderness of a house. There was an old nursery, that had been used for all the little lords and ladies long ago, with a pleasant fire burning in the grate, and the kettle boiling on the hob, and tea-things spread out on the table; and out of that room was the night-nursery, with a little crib for Miss Rosamond close to my bed. And old James called up Dorothy, his wife, to bid us welcome; and both he and she were so hospitable and kind, that by and by Miss Rosamond and me felt quite at home; and by the time tea was over, she was sitting on Dorothy's knee, and chattering away as fast as her little tongue could go. I soon found out that Dorothy was from Westmorland, and that bound her and me together, as it were; and I would never wish to meet with kinder people than were old James and his wife. James had lived pretty nearly all his life in my lord's family, and thought there was no one so grand as they. He even looked down a little on his wife; because, till he had married her, she had never lived in any but a farmer's household. But he was very fond of her, as well he might be. They had one servant under them, to do all the rough work. Agnes they called her; and she and me, and James and Dorothy, with Miss

Furnivall and Mrs. Stark, made up the family; always remembering my sweet little Miss Rosamond! I used to wonder what they had done before she came, they thought so much of her now. Kitchen and drawing-room, it was all the same. The hard, sad Miss Furnivall, and the cold Mrs. Stark, looked pleased when she came fluttering in like a bird, playing and pranking hither and thither, with a continual murmur, and pretty prattle of gladness. I am sure, they were sorry many a time when she flitted away into the kitchen, though they were too proud to ask her to stay with them, and were a little surprised at her taste; though to be sure, as Mrs. Stark said, it was not to be wondered at, remembering what stock her father had come of. The great, old rambling house was a famous place for little Miss Rosamond. She made expeditions all over it, with me at her heels; all, except the east wing, which was never opened, and whither we never thought of going. But in the western and northern part was many a pleasant room; full of things that were curiosities to us, though they might not have been to people who had seen more. The windows were darkened by the sweeping boughs of the trees, and the ivy which had overgrown them: but, in the green gloom, we could manage to see old China jars and carved ivory boxes, and great heavy books, and, above all, the old pictures!

Once, I remember, my darling would have Dorothy go with us to tell us who they all were; for they were all portraits of some of my lord's family, though Dorothy could not tell us the names of every one. We had gone through most of the rooms, when we came to the old state drawing-room over the hall, and there was a picture of Miss Furnivall; or, as she was called in those days, Miss Grace, for she was the younger sister. Such a beauty she must have been! but with such a set, proud look, and such scorn looking out of her handsome eyes, with her eyebrows just a little raised, as if she wondered how any one could have the impertinence to look at her; and her lip curled at us, as we stood there gazing. She had a dress on, the like of which I had never seen before, but it was all the fashion when she was young: a hat of some soft white stuff like beaver, pulled a little over her brows, and a beautiful plume of feathers sweeping round it on one side; and her gown of blue satin was open in front to a quilted white stomacher.

'Well, to be sure!' said I, when I had gazed my fill. 'Flesh is grass, they do say; but who would have thought that Miss Furnivall had been such an out-and-out beauty, to see her now?'

'Yes,' said Dorothy. 'Folks change sadly. But if what my master's father used to say was true, Miss Furnivall, the elder sister, was handsomer than Miss Grace. Her picture is here somewhere; but, if I show it you, you must never let on, even to James, that you have seen it. Can the little lady hold her tongue, think you?' asked she.

I was not so sure, for she was such a little sweet, bold, open-spoken child, so I set her to hide herself; and then I helped Dorothy to turn a great picture, that leaned with its face towards the wall, and was not hung up as the others were. To be sure, it beat Miss Grace for beauty; and, I think, for scornful pride, too, though in that matter it might be hard to choose. I could have looked at it an hour, but Dorothy seemed half frightened at having shown it to me, and hurried it back again, and bade me run and find Miss Rosamond, for that there were some ugly places about the house, where she should like ill for the child to go. I was a brave, high-spirited girl, and thought little of what the old woman said, for I liked hide-and-seek as well as any child in the parish; so off I ran to find my little one.

As winter drew on, and the days grew shorter, I was sometimes almost certain that I heard a noise as if some one was playing on the great organ in the hall. I did not hear it every evening; but, certainly, I did very often; usually when I was sitting with Miss Rosamond, after I had put her to bed, and keeping quite still and silent in the bedroom. Then I used to hear it booming and swelling away in the distance. The first night, when I went down to my supper, I asked Dorothy who had been playing music, and James said very shortly that I was a gowk to take the wind soughing among the trees for music: but I saw Dorothy look at him very fearfully, and Bessy, the kitchen-maid, said something beneath her breath, and went quite white. I saw they did not like my question, so I held my peace till I was with Dorothy alone, when I knew I could get a good deal out of her. So, the next day, I watched my time, and I coaxed and asked her who it was that played the organ; for I knew that it was the organ and not the wind well enough, for all I had kept silence before James. But Dorothy had had her lesson, I'll warrant, and never a word could I get from her. So then I tried Bessy, though I had always held my head rather above her, as I was evened to James and Dorothy, and she was little better than their servant. So she said I must never, never tell; and if I ever told, I was never to say *she* had told me; but it was a very strange noise, and she had heard it many a time, but most of all on winter nights, and before storms; and folks did say, it was the old lord playing on the great organ in the hall, just as he used to do when he was alive; but who the old lord was, or why he played, and why he played on stormy winter evenings in particular, she either could not or would not tell me. Well! I told you I had a brave heart; and I thought it was rather pleasant to have that grand music rolling about the house, let who would be the player; for now it rose above the great gusts of wind, and wailed and triumphed just like a living creature, and then it fell to a softness most complete; only it was always music, and tunes, so it was nonsense to call it the wind. I thought at first that it might be Miss Furnivall who played, unknown to Bessy; but, one day when I was in the hall by myself, I opened the organ and peeped all about it and around it, as I had done to the organ in Crosthwaite Church once before, and I saw it was all broken and destroyed inside, though it looked so brave and fine; and then, though it was noonday, my flesh began to creep a little, and I shut it up, and run away pretty quickly to my own bright nursery; and I did not like hearing the music for some time after that, any more than James and Dorothy did. All this time Miss Rosamond was making herself more and more beloved. The old ladies liked her to dine with them at their early dinner; James stood behind Miss Furnivall's chair, and I behind Miss Rosamond's all in state; and, after dinner, she would play about in a corner of the great drawing-room, as still as any mouse, while Miss Furnivall slept, and I had my dinner in the kitchen. But she was glad enough to come to me in the nursery afterwards; for, as she said, Miss Furnivall was so sad, and Mrs. Stark so dull; but she and I were merry enough; and, by-and-by, I got not to care for that weird rolling music, which did one no harm, if we did not know where it came from.

That winter was very cold. In the middle of October the frosts began, and lasted many, many weeks. I remember, one day at dinner, Miss Furnivall lifted up her sad, heavy eyes, and said to Mrs. Stark, 'I am afraid we shall have a terrible winter,' in a strange kind of meaning way. But Mrs. Stark pretended not to hear, and talked very loud of something else. My little lady and I did not care for the frost; not we! As long as it was dry we climbed up the steep brows, behind the house, and went up on the Fells, which were bleak, and bare enough, and there we ran races in the fresh, sharp air; and once we came down by a new path that took us past the two old gnarled holly-trees, which grew about half-way down by the east side of the house. But the days grew shorter and shorter; and the old lord, if it was he, played away more and more stormily and sadly on the great organ. One Sunday afternoon—it must have been towards the end of November—I asked Dorothy to take charge of little Missey when she came out of the drawing-room, after Miss Furnivall had had her nap; for it was too cold to take her with me to church, and yet I wanted to go. And Dorothy was glad enough to promise, and was so fond of the child that all seemed well; and Bessy and I set off very briskly, though the sky hung heavy and black over the white earth, as if the night had never fully gone away; and the air, though still, was very biting and keen.

'We shall have a fall of snow,' said Bessy to me. And sure enough, even while we were in church, it came down thick, in great large flakes, so thick it almost darkened the windows. It had stopped snowing before we came out, but it lay soft, thick, and deep beneath our feet, as we tramped home. Before we got to the hall the moon rose, and I think it was lighter then—what with the moon, and what with the white dazzling snow—than it had been when we went to church, between two and three o'clock. I have not told you that Miss Furnivall and Mrs. Stark never went to church: they used to read the prayers together, in their quiet gloomy way; they seemed to feel the Sunday very long without their tapestry-work to be busy at. So when I went to Dorothy in the kitchen, to fetch Miss Rosamond and take her upstairs with me, I did not much wonder when the old woman told me that the ladies had kept the child with them, and that she had never come to the kitchen, as I had bidden her, when she was tired to behaving pretty in the drawing-room. So I took off my things and went to find her, and bring her to her supper in the nursery. But when I went into the best drawing-room, there sat the two old ladies, very still and quiet, dropping out a word now and then, but looking as if nothing so bright and merry as Miss Rosamond had ever been near them. Still I thought she might be hiding from me; it was one of her pretty ways; and that she had persuaded them to look as if they knew nothing about her; so I went softly peeping under this sofa, and behind that chair, making believe I was sadly frightened at not finding her.

'What's the matter, Hester?' said Mrs. Stark, sharply. I don't know if Miss Furnivall had seen me, for, as I told you, she was very deaf, and she sat quite still, idly staring into the fire, with her hopeless face. 'I'm only looking for my little Rosy-Posy,' replied I, still thinking that the child was there, and near me, though I could not see her.

'Miss Rosamond is not here,' said Mrs. Stark. 'She went away more than an hour ago to find Dorothy.' And she too turned and went on looking into the fire.

My heart sank at this, and I began to wish I had never left my darling. I went back to Dorothy and told her. James was gone out for the day, but she and me and Bessy took lights and went up into the nursery first, and then we roamed over the great large house, calling and entreating Miss Rosamond to come out of her hiding-place, and not frighten us to death in that way. But there was no answer; no sound.

'Oh!' said I at last, 'Can she have got into the east wing and hidden there?'

But Dorothy said it was not possible, for that she herself had never been in there; that the doors were always locked, and my lord's steward had the keys, she believed; at any rate, neither she nor James had ever seen them: so I said I would go back, and see if, after all, she was not hidden in the drawing-room, unknown to the old ladies; and if I found her there, I said, I would whip her well for the fright she had given me; but I never meant to do it. Well, I went back to the west drawing-room, and I told Mrs. Stark we could not find her anywhere, and asked for leave to look all about the furniture there, for I thought now, that she might have fallen asleep in some warm hidden corner; but no! we looked, Miss Furnivall got up and looked, trembling all over, and she was nowhere there; then we set off again, every one in the house, and looked in all the places we had searched before, but we could not find her. Miss Furnivall shivered and shook so much, that Mrs. Stark took her back into the warm drawing-room; but not before they had made me promise to bring her to them when she was found. Well-a-day! I began to think she never would be found, when I be-thought me to look out into the great front court, all covered with snow. I was upstairs when I looked out; but, it was such clear moonlight, I could see, quite plain, two little footprints, which might be traced from the hall door, and round the corner of the east wing. I don't know how I got down, but I tugged open the great, stiff hall door; and, throwing the skirt of my gown over my head for a cloak, I ran out. I turned the east corner, and there a black shadow fell on the snow; but when I came again into the moonlight, there were the little footmarks going up—up to the Fells. It was bitter cold; so cold that the air almost took the skin off my face as I ran, but I ran on, crying to think how my poor little darling must be perished, and frightened. I was within sight to the holly-trees when I saw a shepherd coming down the hill, bearing something in his arms wrapped in his maud. He shouted to me, and asked me if I had lost a bairn; and, when I could not speak for crying, he bore towards me, and I saw my wee bairnie lying still, and white, and stiff, in his arms, as if she had been dead. He told me he had been up the Fells to gather in his sheep, before the deep cold of night came on, and that under the holly-trees (black marks on the hill-side, where no other bush was for miles around) he had found my little lady—my lamb—my queen—my darling—stiff and cold, in the terrible sleep which is frost-begotten. Oh! the joy, and the tears of having her in my arms once again! for I would not let him carry her; but took her, maud and all, into my own arms, and held her near my own warm neck and heart, and felt the life stealing slowly back again into her little gentle limbs. But she was still insensible when we reached the hall, and I had no breath for speech. We went in by the kitchen door.

'Bring the warming-pan,' said I; and I carried her upstairs and began undressing her by the nursery fire, which Bessy had kept up. I called my little lammie all the sweet and playful names I could think of—even while my eyes were blinded by my tears; and at last, oh! at length she opened her large blue eyes. Then I put her into her warm bed, and sent Dorothy down to tell Miss Furnivall that all was well; and I made up my mind to sit by my darling's bedside the live-long night. She fell away into a soft sleep as soon as her pretty head had touched the pillow, and I watched by her till morning light; when she wakened up bright and clear—or so I thought at first—and, my dears, so I think now.

She said that she had fancied that she should like to go to Dorothy, for that both the old ladies were asleep, and it was very dull in the drawing-room; and that, as she was going through the west lobby, she saw the snow through the high window falling—falling—soft and steady; but she wanted to see it lying pretty and white on the ground; so she made her way into the great hall; and then, going to the window, she saw it bright and soft upon the drive; but while she stood there, she saw a little girl, not so old as she was, 'but so pretty,' said my darling, 'and this little girl beckoned to me to come out; and oh, she was so pretty and so sweet, I could not choose but go.' And then this other little girl had taken her by the hand, and side by side the two had gone round the east corner.

'Now, you are a naughty little girl, and telling stories,' said I. 'What would your good mamma, that is in heaven, and never told a story in her life, say to her little Rosamond, if she heard her—and I dare say she does—telling stories!'

'Indeed, Hester,' sobbed out my child, 'I'm telling you true. Indeed I am.'

'Don't tell me!' said I, very stern. 'I tracked you by your footmarks through the snow; there were only yours to be seen: and if you had had a little girl to go hand-in-hand with you up the hill, don't you think the footprints would have gone along with yours?'

'I can't help it, dear, dear Hester,' said she, crying, 'if they did not; I never looked at her feet, but she held my hand fast and tight in her little one, and it was very, very cold. She took me up the Fell-path, up to the holly trees; and there I saw a lady weeping and crying; but when she saw me, she hushed her weeping, and smiled very proud and grand, and took me on her knee, and began to lull me to sleep; and that's all, Hester—but that is true; and my dear mamma knows it is,' said she, crying. So I thought the child was in a fever, and pretended to believe her, as she went over her story —over and over again, and always the same. At last Dorothy knocked at the door with Miss Rosamond's breakfast; and she told me the old ladies were down in the eating parlour, and that they wanted to speak to me. They had both been into the night-nursery the evening before, but it was after Miss Rosamond was asleep; so they had only looked at her—not asked me any questions.

'I shall catch it,' thought I to myself, as I went along the north gallery. 'And yet,' I thought, taking courage, 'it was in their charge I left her; and it's they that's to blame for letting her steal away unknown and unwatched.' So I went in boldly, and told my story. I told it all to Miss Furnivall, shouting it close to her ear; but when I came to the mention of the other little girl out in the snow, coaxing and tempting her out, and wiling her up to the grand and beautiful lady by the holly-tree, she threw her arms up—her old and withered arms—and cried aloud, 'Oh! Heaven, forgive! Have mercy!'

Mrs. Stark took hold of her; roughly enough, I thought; but she was past Mrs. Stark's management, and spoke to me, in a kind of wild warning and authority.

'Hester! keep her from that child! It will lure her to her death! That evil child! Tell her it is a wicked, naughty child.' Then Mrs. Stark hurried me out of the room; where, indeed, I was glad enough to go; but Miss Furnivall kept shrieking out, 'Oh! have mercy! Wilt Thou never forgive! It is many a long year ago'—

I was very uneasy in my mind after that. I durst never leave Miss Rosamond, night or day, for fear lest she might slip off again, after some fancy or other; and all the more, because I thought I could make out that Miss Furnivall was crazy, from their odd ways about her; and I was afraid lest something of the same kind (which might be in the family, you know) hung over my darling. And the great frost never ceased all this time; and, whenever it was a more stormy night than usual, between the gusts, and through the wind, we heard the old lord playing on the great organ. But, old lord, or not, wherever Miss Rosamond went, there I followed; for my love for her, pretty helpless orphan, was stronger than my fear for the grand and terrible sound. Besides, it rested with me to keep her cheerful and merry, as beseemed her age. So we played together, and wandered together, here and there, and everywhere; for I never dared to lose sight of her again in that large and rambling house. And so it happened, that one afternoon, not long before Christmas Day, we were playing together on the billiard-table in the great hall (not that we knew the right way of playing, but she liked to roll the smooth ivory balls with her pretty hands, and I liked to do whatever she did); and, by-and-by, without our noticing it, it grew dusk indoors, though it was still light in the open air, and I was thinking of taking her back into the nursery, when, all of a sudden, she cried out:

'Look, Hester! look! there is my poor little girl out in the snow!'

I turned towards the long narrow windows, and there, sure enough, I saw a little girl, less than my Miss Rosamond—dressed all unfit to be out-of-doors such a bitter night—crying, and beating against the window-panes, as if she wanted to be let in. She seemed to sob and wail, till Miss Rosamond could bear it no longer, and was flying to the door to open it, when, all of a sudden, and close upon us, the great organ pealed out so loud and thundering, it fairly made me tremble; and all the more, when I remembered me that, even in the stillness of that dead-cold weather, I had heard no sound of little battering hands upon the window-glass, although the Phantom Child had seemed to put forth all its force; and, although I had seen it wail and cry, no faintest touch of sound had fallen upon my ears. Whether I remembered all this at the very moment, I do not know; the great organ sound had so stunned me into terror; but this I know, I caught up Miss Rosamond before she got the hall-door opened, and clutched her, and carried her away, kicking and screaming, into the large bright kitchen, where Dorothy and Agnes were busy with their mince-pies.

'What is the matter with my sweet one?' cried Dorothy, as I bore in Miss Rosamond, who was sobbing as if her heart would break.

'She won't let me open the door for my little girl to come in; and she'll die if she is out on the Fells all night. Cruel, naughty Hester,' she said, slapping me; but she might have struck harder, for I had seen a look of ghastly terror on Dorothy's face, which made my very blood run cold.

'Shut the back-kitchen door fast, and bolt it well,' said she to Agnes. She said no more; she gave me raisins and almonds to quiet Miss Rosamond: but she sobbed about the little girl in the snow, and would not touch any of the good things. I was thankful when she cried herself to sleep in bed. Then I stole down to the kitchen, and told Dorothy I had made up my mind. I would carry my darling back to my father's house in Applethwaite; where, if we lived humbly, we lived at peace. I said I had been frightened enough with the old lord's organ-playing; but now, that I had seen for myself this little moaning child, all decked out as no child in the neighbourhood could be, beating and battering to get in, yet always without any sound or noise—with the dark wound on its right shoulder; and that Miss Rosamond had known it again for the phantom that had nearly lured her to her death (which Dorothy knew was true); I would stand it no longer.

I saw Dorothy change colour once or twice. When I had done, she told me she did not think I could take Miss Rosamond with me, for that she was my lord's ward, and I had no right over her; and she asked me, would I leave the child that I was so fond of, just for sounds and sights that could do me no harm; and that they had all had to get used to in their turns? I was all in a hot, trembling passion; and I said it was very well for her to talk, that knew what these sights and noises betokened, and that had, perhaps, had something to do with the Spectre-Child while it was alive. And I taunted her so, that she told me all she knew, at last; and then I wished I had never been told, for it only made me more afraid than ever.

She said she had heard the tale from old neighbours, that were alive when she was first married; when folks used to come to the hall sometimes, before it had got such a bad name on the country side; it might not be true, or it might, what she had been told.

The old lord was Miss Furnivall's father—Miss Grace, as Dorothy called her, for Miss Maude was the elder, and Miss Furnivall by rights. The old lord was eaten up with pride. Such a proud man was never seen or heard of; and his daughters were like him. No one was good enough to wed them, although they had choice enough; for they were the great beauties of their day, as I had seen by their portraits, where they hung in the state drawing-room. But, as the old saying is, 'Pride will have a fall'; and these two haughty beauties fell in love with the same man, and he no better than a foreign musician, whom their father had down from London to play music with him at the Manor House. For, above all things, next to his pride, the old lord loved music. He could play on nearly every instrument that ever was heard of: and it was a strange thing it did not soften him; but he was a fierce dour old man, and had broken his poor wife's heart with his cruelty, they said. He was mad after music, and would pay any money for it. So he got this foreigner to come; who made such beautiful music, that they said the very birds on the trees stopped their singing to listen. And, by degrees, this foreign gentleman got such a hold over the old lord, that nothing would serve him but that he must come every year; and it was he that had the great organ brought from Holland, and built up in the hall, where it stood now. He taught the old lord to play on it; but many and many a time, when Lord Furnivall was thinking of nothing but his fine organ, and his finer music, the dark foreigner was walking abroad in the woods with one of the young ladies; now Miss Maude, and then Miss Grace.

Miss Maude won the day and carried off the prize, such as it was; and he and she were married, all unknown to any one; and before he made his next yearly visit, she had been confined of a little girl at a farmhouse on the Moors, while her father and Miss Grace thought she was away at Doncaster Races. But though she was a wife and a mother, she was not a bit softened, but as haughty and as passionate as ever; and perhaps more so, for she was jealous of Miss Grace, to whom her foreign husband paid a deal of court—by way of blinding her—as he told his wife. But Miss Grace triumphed over Miss Maude, and Miss Maude grew fiercer and fiercer, both with her husband and with her sister; and the former—who could easily shake off what was disagreeable, and hide himself in foreign countries—went away a month before his usual time that summer, and half-threatened that he would never come back again. Meanwhile, the little girl was left at the farm-house, and her mother used to have her horse saddled and gallop wildly over the hills to see her once every week, at the very least—for where she loved, she loved; and where she hated, she hated. And the old lord went on playing—playing on his organ; and the servants thought the sweet music he made had soothed down his awful temper, of which (Dorothy said) some terrible tales could be told. He grew infirm too, and had to walk with a crutch; and his son—that was the present Lord Furnivall's father—was with the army in America, and the other son at sea; so Miss Maude had it pretty much her own way, and she and Miss Grace grew colder and bitterer to each other every day; till at last they hardly ever spoke, except when the old lord was by. The foreign musician came again the next summer, but it was for the last time; for they led him such a life with their jealousy and their passions, that he grew weary, and went away, and never was heard of again. And Miss Maude, who had always meant to have her marriage acknowledged when her father should be dead, was left now a deserted wife—whom nobody knew to have been married—with a child that she dared not own, although she loved it to distraction; living with a father whom she feared, and a sister whom she hated. When the next summer passed over and the dark foreigner never came, both Miss Maude and Miss Grace grew gloomy and sad; they had a haggard look about them, though they looked handsome as ever. But by-and-by Miss Maude brightened; for her father grew more and more infirm, and more than ever carried away by his music; and she and Miss Grace lived almost entirely apart, having separate rooms, the one on the west side, Miss Maude on the east—those very rooms which were now shut up. So she thought she might have her little girl with her, and no one need ever know except those who dared not speak about it, and were bound to believe that it was, as she said, a cottager's child she had taken a fancy to. All this, Dorothy said, was pretty well known; but what came afterwards no one knew, except Miss Grace, and Mrs. Stark, who was even then her maid, and much more of a friend to her than ever her sister had been. But the servants supposed, from words that were dropped, that Miss Maude had triumphed over Miss Grace, and told her that all the time the dark foreigner had been mocking her with pretended love—he was her own husband; the colour left Miss Grace's cheek and lips that very day for ever, and she was heard to say many a time that sooner or later she would have her revenge; and Mrs. Stark was for ever spying about the east rooms.

One fearful night, just after the New Year had come in, when the snow was lying thick and deep, and the flakes were still falling—fast enough to blind any one who might be out and abroad—there was a great and violent noise heard, and the old lord's voice above all, cursing and swearing awfully—and the cries of a little child—and the proud defiance of a fierce woman—and the sound of a blow—and a dead stillness—and moans and wailings dying away on the hill-side! Then the old lord summoned all his servants, and told them, with terrible oaths, and words more terrible, that his daughter had disgraced herself, and that he had turned her out of doors—her, and her child—and that if ever they gave her help—or food—or shelter—he prayed that they might never enter Heaven. And, all the while, Miss Grace stood by him, white and still as any stone; and when he had ended she heaved a great sigh, as much as to say her work was done, and her end was accomplished. But the old lord never touched his organ again, and died within the year; and no wonder! for, on the morrow of that wild and fearful night, the shepherds, coming down the Fell side, found Miss Maude sitting, all crazy and smiling, under the holly-trees, nursing a dead child—with a terrible mark on its right shoulder. 'But that was not what killed it,' said Dorothy; 'it was the frost and the cold;—every wild creature was in its hole, and every beast in its fold—while the child and its mother were turned out to wander on the Fells! And now you know all! and I wonder if you are less frightened now?'

I was more frightened than ever; but I said I was not. I wished Miss Rosamond and myself well out of that dreadful house for ever; but I would not leave her, and I dared not take her away. But oh! how I watched her, and guarded her! We bolted the doors, and shut the window-shutters fast, an hour or more before dark, rather than leave them open five minutes too late. But my little lady still heard the weird child crying and mourning; and not all we could do or say could keep her from wanting to go to her, and let her in from the cruel wind and the snow. All this time, I kept away from Miss Furnivall and Mrs. Stark, as much as ever I could; for I feared them—I knew no good could be about them, with their grey hard faces, and their dreamy eyes, looking back into the ghastly years that were gone. But, even in my fear, I had a kind of pity—for Miss Furnivall, at least. Those gone down to the pit can hardly have a more hopeless look than that which was ever on her face. At last I even got so sorry for her—who never said a word but what was quite forced from her—that I prayed for her; and I taught Miss Rosamond to pray for one who had done a deadly sin; but often when she came to those words, she would listen, and start up from her knees, and say, 'I hear my little girl plaining and crying very sad—Oh! let her in, or she will die!'

One night—just after New Year's Day had come at last, and the long winter had taken a turn, as I hoped—I heard the west drawing-room bell ring three times, which was the signal for me. I would not leave Miss Rosamond alone, for all she was asleep—for the old lord had been playing wilder than ever—and I feared lest my darling should waken to hear the spectre child; see her I knew she could not. I had fastened the windows too well for that. So I took her out of her bed and wrapped her up in such outer clothes as were most handy, and carried her down to the drawing-room, where the old ladies sat at their tapestry work as usual. They looked up when I came in, and Mrs. Stark asked, quite astounded, 'Why did I bring Miss Rosamond there, out of her warm bed?' I had begun to whisper, 'Because I was afraid of her being tempted out while I was away, by the wild child in the snow,' when she stopped me short (with a glance at Miss Furnivall), and said Miss Furnivall wanted me to undo some work she had done wrong, and which neither of them could see to unpick. So I laid my pretty dear on the sofa, and sat down on a stool by them, and hardened my heart against them, as I heard the wind rising and howling.

Miss Rosamond slept on sound, for all the wind blew so; and Miss Furnivall said never a word, nor looked round when the gusts shook the windows. All at once she started up to her full height, and put up one hand, as if to bid us listen.

'I hear voices!' said she. 'I hear terrible screams—I hear my father's voice!'

Just at that moment my darling wakened with a sudden start: 'My little girl is crying, oh, how she is crying!' and she tried to get up and go to her, but she got her feet entangled in the blanket, and I caught her up; for my flesh had begun to creep at these noises, which they heard while we could catch no sound. In a minute or two the noises came, and gathered fast, and filled our ears; we, too, heard voices and screams, and no longer heard the winter's wind that raged abroad. Mrs. Stark looked at me, and I at her, but we dared not speak. Suddenly Miss Furnivall went towards the door, out into the ante-room, through the west lobby, and opened the door into the great hall. Mrs. Stark followed, and I durst not be left, though my heart almost stopped beating for fear. I wrapped my darling tight in my arms, and went out with them. In the hall the screams were louder than ever; they sounded to come from the east wing—nearer and nearer—close on the other side of the locked-up doors—close behind them. Then I noticed that the great bronze chandelier seemed all alight, though the hall was dim, and that a fire was blazing in the vast hearth-place, though it gave no heat; and I shuddered up with terror, and folded my darling closer to me. But as I did so, the east door shook, and she, suddenly struggling to get free from me, cried, 'Hester! I must go! My little girl is there; I hear her; she is coming! Hester, I must go!'

I held her tight with all my strength; with a set will, I held her. If I had died, my hands would have grasped her still, I was so resolved in my mind. Miss Furnivall stood listening, and paid no regard to my darling, who had got down to the ground, and whom I, upon my knees now, was holding with both my arms clasped round her neck; she still striving and crying to get free.

All at once the east door gave way with a thundering crash, as if torn open in a violent passion, and there came into that broad and mysterious light, the figure of a tall old man, with grey hair and gleaming eyes. He drove before him, with many a relentless gesture of abhorrence, a stern and beautiful woman, with a little child clinging to her dress.

'O Hester! Hester!' cried Miss Rosamond. 'It's the lady! the lady below the holly-trees; and my little girl is with her. Hester! Hester! let me go to her; they are drawing me to them. I feel them—I feel them. I must go!'

Again she was almost convulsed by her efforts to get away; but I held her tighter and tighter, till I feared I should do her a hurt; but rather that than let her go towards those terrible phantoms. They passed along towards the great hall-door, where the winds howled and ravened for their prey; but before they reached that, the lady turned; and I could see that she defied the old man with a fierce and proud defiance; but then she quailed—and then she threw up her arms wildly and piteously to save her child—her little child—from a blow from his uplifted crutch.

And Miss Rosamond was torn as by a power stronger than mine, and writhed in my arms, and sobbed (for by this time the poor darling was growing faint).

'They want me to go with them on to the Fells—they are drawing me to them. Oh, my little girl! I would come, but cruel, wicked Hester holds me very tight.' But when she saw the uplifted crutch she swooned away, and I thanked God for it. Just at this moment—when the tall old man, his hair streaming as in the blast of a furnace, was going to strike the little shrinking child—Miss Furnivall, the old woman by my side, cried out, 'Oh, father! father! spare the little innocent child!' But just then I saw—we all saw—another phantom shape itself, and grow clear out of the blue and misty light that filled the hall; we had not seen her till now, for it was another lady who stood by the old man, with a look of relentless hate and triumphant scorn. That figure was very beautiful to look upon, with a soft white hat drawn down over the proud brows, and a red and curling lip. It was dressed in an open robe of blue satin. I had seen that figure before. It was the likeness of Miss Furnivall in her youth; and the terrible phantoms moved on, regardless of old Miss Furnivall's wild entreaty—and the uplifted crutch fell on the right shoulder of the little child, and the younger sister looked on, stony and deadly serene. But at that moment, the dim lights, and the fire that gave no heat, went out of themselves, and Miss Furnivall lay at our feet stricken down by the palsy—death-stricken.

Yes! she was carried to her bed that night never to rise again. She lay with her face to the wall, muttering low but muttering alway: 'Alas! alas! what is done in youth can never be undone in age! What is done in youth can never be undone in age!'

A Manchester Marriage By Elizabeth Gaskell

Mr and Mrs Openshaw came from Manchester to settle in London. He had been, what is called in Lancashire, a salesman for a large manufacturing firm, who were extending their business, and opening a warehouse in the city; where Mr Openshaw was now to superintend their affairs. He rather enjoyed the change; having a kind of curiosity about London, which he had never yet been able to gratify in his brief visits to the metropolis. At the same time, he had an odd, shrewd contempt for the inhabitants, whom he always pictured to himself as fine, lazy people, caring nothing but for fashion and aristocracy, and lounging away their days in Bond Street, and such places; ruining good English, and ready in their turn to despise him as a provincial. The hours that the men of business kept in the city scandalized him too, accustomed as he was to the early dinners of Manchester folk and the consequently far longer evenings. Still, he was pleased to go to London, though he would not for the world have confessed it, even to himself, and always spoke of the step to his friends as one demanded of him by the interests of his employers, and sweetened to him by a considerable increase of salary. This, indeed, was so liberal that he might have been justified in taking a much larger house than the one he did, had he not thought himself bound to set an example to Londoners of how little a Manchester man of business cared for show. Inside, however, he furnished it with an unusual degree of comfort, and, in the winter-time, he insisted on keeping up as large fires as the grates would allow, in every room where the temperature was in the least chilly. Moreover, his northern sense of hospitality was such that, if he were at home, he could hardly suffer a visitor to leave the house without forcing meat and drink upon him. Every servant in the house was well warmed, well fed, and kindly treated; for their master scorned all petty saving in aught that conduced to comfort; while he amused himself by following out all his accustomed habits and individual ways, in defiance of what any of his new neighbours might think.

His wife was a pretty, gentle woman, of suitable age and character. He was forty-two, she thirty-five. He was loud and decided; she soft and yielding. They had two children; or rather, I should say, she had two; for the elder, a girl of eleven, was Mrs Openshaw's child by Frank Wilson, her first husband. The younger was a little boy, Edwin, who could just prattle, and to whom his father delighted to speak in the broadest and most unintelligible Lancashire dialect, in order to keep up what he called the true Saxon accent.

Mrs Openshaw's Christian name was Alice, and her first husband had been her own cousin. She was the orphan niece of a sea-captain in Liverpool; a quiet, grave little creature, of great personal attraction when she was fifteen or sixteen, with regular features and a blooming complexion. But she was very shy, and believed herself to be very stupid and awkward; and was frequently scolded by her aunt, her own uncle's second wife. So when her cousin, Frank Wilson, came home from a long absence at sea, and first was kind and protective to her; secondly, attentive; and thirdly, desperately in love with her, she hardly knew how to be grateful enough to him. It is true, she would have preferred his remaining in the first or second stages of behaviour; for his violent love puzzled and frightened her. Her uncle neither helped nor hindered the love affair, though it was going on under his own eyes. Frank's stepmother had such a variable temper, that there was no knowing whether what she liked one day she would like the next, or not. At length she went to such extremes of crossness that Alice was only too glad to shut her eyes and rush blindly at the chance of escape from domestic tyranny offered her by a marriage with her cousin; and, liking him better than any one in the world, except her uncle (who was at this time at sea), she went off one morning and was married to him, her only bridesmaid being the housemaid at her aunt's. The consequence was that Frank and his wife went into lodgings, and Mrs Wilson refused to see them, and turned away Norah, the warm-hearted housemaid, whom they accordingly took into their service. When Captain Wilson returned from his voyage he was very cordial with the young couple, and spent many an evening at their lodgings, smoking his pipe and sipping his grog; but he told them, for quietness' sake, he could not ask them to his own house; for his wife was bitter against them. They were not, however, very unhappy about this.

The seed of future unhappiness lay rather in Frank's vehement, passionate disposition, which led him to resent his wife's shyness and want of demonstrativeness as failures in conjugal duty. He was already tormenting himself, and her too in a slighter degree, by apprehensions and imaginations of what might befall her during his approaching absence at sea. At last, he went to his father and urged him to insist upon Alice's being once more received under his roof; the more especially as there was now a prospect of her confinement while her husband was away on his voyage. Captain Wilson was, as he himself expressed it, 'breaking up', and unwilling to undergo the excitement of a scene; yet he felt that what his son said was true. So he went to his wife. And before Frank set sail, he had the comfort of seeing his wife installed in her old little garret in his father's house. To have placed her in the one best spare room was a step beyond Mrs Wilson's powers of submission or generosity. The worst part about it, however, was that the faithful Norah had to be dismissed. Her place as housemaid had been filled up; and, even if it had not, she had forfeited Mrs Wilson's good opinion for ever. She comforted her young master and mistress by pleasant prophecies of the time when they would have a household of their own; of which, whatever service she might be in meanwhile, she should be sure to form a part. Almost the last action Frank did, before setting sail, was going with Alice to see Norah once more at her mother's house; and then he went away.

Alice's father-in-law grew more and more feeble as winter advanced. She was of great use to her stepmother in nursing and amusing him; and although there was anxiety enough in the household, there was, perhaps, more of peace than there had been for years, for Mrs Wilson had not a bad heart, and was softened by the visible approach of death to one whom she loved, and touched by the lonely condition of the young creature expecting her first confinement in her husband's absence. To this relenting mood Norah owed the permission to come and nurse Alice when her baby was born, and to remain and attend on Captain Wilson.

Before one letter had been received from Frank (who had sailed for the East Indies and China), his father died. Alice was always glad to remember that he had held her baby in his arms, and kissed and blessed it before his death. After that, and the consequent examination into the state of his affairs, it was found that he had left far less property than people had been led by his style of living to expect; and what money there was, was settled all upon his wife, and at her disposal after her death. This did not signify much to Alice, as Frank was now first mate of his ship, and, in another voyage or two, would be captain.

Meanwhile he had left her rather more than two hundred pounds (all his savings) in the bank.

It became time for Alice to hear from her husband. One letter from the Cape she had already received. The next was to announce his arrival in India. As week after week passed over, and no intelligence of the ship having got there reached the office of the owners, and the captain's wife was in the same state of ignorant suspense as Alice herself, her fears grew most oppressive. At length the day came when, in reply to her inquiry at the shipping office, they told her that the owners had given up hope of ever hearing more of the Betsy-Jane and had sent in their claim upon the underwriters. Now that he was gone for ever, she first felt a yearning, longing love for the kind cousin, the dear friend, the sympathizing protector, whom she should never see again; first felt a passionate desire to show him his child, whom she had hitherto rather craved to have all to herself, her own sole possession. Her grief was, however, noiseless and quiet - rather to the scandal of Mrs Wilson who bewailed her stepson as if he and she had always lived together in perfect harmony, and who evidently thought it her duty to burst into fresh tears at every strange face she saw; dwelling on his poor young widow's desolate state, and the helplessness of the fatherless child, with an unction as if she liked the excitement of the sorrowful story.

So passed away the first days of Alice's widowhood. By and by things subsided into their natural and tranquil course. But, as if the young creature was always to be in some heavy trouble, her ewe-lamb began to be ailing, pining, and sickly. The child's mysterious illness turned out to be some affection of the spine, likely to affect health but not to shorten life at least, so the doctors said. But the long, dreary suffering of one whom a mother loves as Alice loved her only child, is hard to look forward to. Only Norah guessed what Alice suffered; no one but God knew.

And so it fell out, that when Mrs Wilson, the elder, came to her one day, in violent distress, occasioned by a very material diminution in the value of the property that her husband had left her a diminution which made her income barely enough to support herself, much less Alice the latter could hardly understand how anything which did not touch health or life could cause such grief; and she received the intelligence with irritating composure. But when, that afternoon, the little sick child was brought in, and the grandmother who, after all, loved it well began a fresh moan over her losses to its unconscious ears saying how she had planned to consult this or that doctor, and to give it this or that comfort or luxury in after years, but that now all chance of this had passed away. Alice's heart was touched, and she drew near to Mrs Wilson with unwonted caresses, and, in a spirit not unlike to that of Ruth, entreated that, come what would, they might remain together. After much discussion in succeeding days, it was arranged that Mrs Wilson should take a house in Manchester, furnishing it partly with what furniture she had, and providing the rest with Alice's remaining two hundred pounds. Mrs Wilson was herself a Manchester woman, and naturally longed to return to her native town; some connexions of her own, too, at that time required lodgings, for which they were willing to pay pretty handsomely. Alice undertook the active superintendence and superior work of the household; Norah; willing, faithful Norah offered to cook, scour, do anything in short, so that she might but remain with them.

The plan succeeded. For some years their first lodgers remained with them, and all went smoothly with that one sad exception of the little girl's increasing deformity. How that mother loved that child, it is not for words to tell!

Then came a break of misfortune. Their lodgers left, and no one succeeded to them. After some months, it became necessary to remove to a smaller house; and Alice's tender conscience was torn by the idea that she ought not to be a burden to her mother-in-law, but to go out and seek her own maintenance. And leave her child! The thought came like the sweeping boom of a funeral-bell over her heart.

By and by, Mr Openshaw came to lodge with them. He had started in life as the errand-boy and sweeper-out of a warehouse; had struggled up through all the grades of employment in it, fighting his way through the hard, striving Manchester life with strong, pushing energy of character. Every spare moment of time had been sternly given up to self-teaching. He was a capital accountant, a good French and German scholar, a keen, far-seeing tradesman, understanding markets and the bearing of events, both near and distant, on trade; and yet, with such vivid attention to present details, that I do not think he ever saw a group of flowers in the fields without thinking whether their colour would, or would not, form harmonious contrasts in the coming spring muslins and prints. He went to debating societies, and threw himself with all his heart and soul into politics; esteeming, it must be owned, every man a fool or a knave who differed from him, and overthrowing his opponents rather by the loud strength of his language than the calm strength of his logic. There was something of the Yankee in all this. Indeed, his theory ran parallel to the famous Yankee motto 'England flogs creation, and Manchester flogs England.' Such a man, as may be fancied, had had no time for falling in love, or any such nonsense. At the age when most young men go through their courting and matrimony, he had not the means of keeping a wife, and was far too practical to think of having one. And now that he was in easy circumstances, a rising man, he considered women almost as encumbrances to the world, with whom a man had better have as little to do as possible. His first impression of Alice was indistinct, and he did not care enough about her to make it distinct. 'A pretty, yea-nay kind of woman', would have been his description of her, if he had been pushed into a corner. He was rather afraid, in the beginning, that her quiet ways arose from a listlessness and laziness of character, which would have been exceedingly discordant to his active, energetic nature. But, when he found out the punctuality with which his wishes were attended to, and her work was done; when he was called in the morning at the very stroke of the clock, his shaving-water scalding hot, his fire bright, his coffee made exactly as his peculiar fancy dictated (for he was a man who had his theory about everything based upon what he knew of science, and often perfectly original) then he began to think: not that Alice had any particular merit, but that he had got into remarkably good lodgings; his restlessness wore away, and he began to consider himself as almost settled for life in them.

Mr Openshaw had been too busy, all his days, to be introspective. He did not know that he had any tenderness in his nature; and if he had become conscious of its abstract existence he would have considered it as a manifestation of disease in some part of him. But he was decoyed into pity unawares; and pity led on to tenderness. That little helpless child, always carried about by one of the three busy women of the house, or else patiently threading coloured beads in the chair from which, by no effort of its own, could it ever move, the great grave blue eyes, full of serious, not uncheerful, expression, giving to the small delicate face a look beyond its years, the soft plaintive voice dropping out but few words, so unlike the continual prattle of a child caught Mr Openshaw's attention in spite of himself. One day, he half scorned himself for doing so, he cut short his dinner-hour to go in search of some toy, which should take the place of those eternal beads. I forget what he bought; but, when he gave the present (which he took care to do in a short abrupt manner, and when no one was by to see him), he was almost thrilled by the flash of delight that came over that child's face, and he could not help, all through that afternoon, going over and over again the picture left on his memory, by the bright effect of unexpected joy on the little girl's face. When he returned home, he found his slippers placed by his sitting-room fire; and even more careful attention paid to his fancies than was habitual in those model lodgings. When Alice had taken the last of his tea-things away, she had been silent as usual till then, she stood for an instant with the door in her hand. Mr Openshaw looked as if he were deep in his book, though in fact he did not see a line; but was heartily wishing the woman would go, and not make any palaver of gratitude. But she only said:

'I am very much obliged to you, sir. Thank you very much,' and was gone, even before he could send her away with a 'There, my good woman, that's enough!'

For some time longer he took no apparent notice of the child. He even hardened his heart into disregarding her sudden flush of colour and little timid smile of recognition, when he saw her by chance. But, after all, this could not last for ever; and, having a second time given way to tenderness, there was no relapse. The insidious enemy having thus entered his heart, in the guise of compassion to the child, soon assumed the more dangerous form of interest in the mother. He was aware of this change of feeling, despised himself for it, struggled with it; nay, internally yielded to it and cherished it, long before he suffered the slightest expression of it, by word, action, or look to escape him. He watched Alice's docile, obedient ways to her stepmother; the love which she had inspired in the rough Norah (roughened by the wear and tear of sorrow and years); but, above all, he saw the wild, deep, passionate affection existing between her and her child. They spoke little to anyone else, or when anyone else was by; but, when alone together, they talked, and murmured, and cooed, and chattered so continually, that Mr Openshaw first wondered what they could find to say to each other, and next became irritated because they were always so grave and silent with him. All this time he was perpetually devising small new pleasures for the child. His thoughts ran, in a pertinacious way, upon the desolate life before her; and often he came back from his day's work loaded with the very thing Alice had been longing for, but had not been able to procure. One time, it was a little chair for drawing the little sufferer along the streets; and, many an evening that following summer, Mr Openshaw drew her along himself, regardless of the remarks of his acquaintances. One day in autumn, he put down his newspaper, as Alice came in with the breakfast, and said, in as indifferent a voice as he could assume:

'Mrs Frank, is there any reason why we two should not put up our horses together?'

Alice stood still in perplexed wonder. What did he mean? He had resumed the reading of his newspaper, as if he did not expect any answer; so she found silence her safest course, and went on quietly arranging his breakfast, without another word passing between them. Just as he was leaving the house, to go to the warehouse as usual, he turned back and put his head into the bright, neat, tidy kitchen, where all the women breakfasted in the morning:

'You'll think of what I said, Mrs Frank' (this was her name with the lodgers), 'and let me have your opinion upon it tonight.' Alice was thankful that her mother and Norah were too busy talking together to attend much to this speech. She determined not to think about it at all through the day; and, of course, the effort not to think made her think all the more. At night she sent up Norah with his tea. But Mr Openshaw almost knocked Norah down as she was going out at the door, by pushing past her and calling out, 'Mrs Frank!' in an impatient voice, at the top of the stairs. Alice went up, rather than seem to have affixed too much meaning to his words. 'Well, Mrs Frank,' he said, 'what answer? Don't make it too long; for I have lots of office work to get through tonight.'

'I hardly know what you meant, sir,' said truthful Alice.

'Well! I should have thought you might have guessed. You're not new at this sort of work, and I am. However, I'll make it plain this time. Will you have me to be thy wedded husband, and serve me, and love me, and honour me, and all that sort of thing? Because, if you will, I will do as much by you, and be a father to your child and that's more than is put in the prayer-book. Now, I'm a man of my word; and what I say, I feel; and what I promise, I'll do. Now, for your answer!'

Alice was silent. He began to make the tea, as if her reply was a matter of perfect indifference to him; but, as soon as that was done, he became impatient.

'Well?' said he.

'How long, sir, may I have to think over it?'

'Three minutes!' (looking at his watch). 'You've had two already, that makes five. Be a sensible woman, say Yes, and sit down to tea with me, and we'll talk it over together; for, after tea, I shall be busy; say No' (he hesitated a moment to try and keep his voice in the same tone), 'and I shan't say another word about it, but pay up a year's rent for my rooms tomorrow, and be off. Time's up! Yes or no?'

'If you please, sir, you have been so good to little Ailsie -'

'There, sit down comfortably by me on the sofa, and let's have our tea together. I am glad to find you are as good and sensible as I took you for.'

And this was Alice Wilson's second wooing.

Mr Openshaw's will was too strong, and his circumstances too good, for him not to carry all before him. He settled Mrs Wilson in a comfortable house of her own, and made her quite independent of lodgers. The little that Alice said with regard to future plans was in Norah's behalf.

'No,' said Mr Openshaw. 'Norah shall take care of the old lady as long as she lives; and, after that, she shall either come and live with us, or, if she likes it better, she shall have a provision for life for your sake, missus. No one who has been good to you or the child shall go unrewarded. But even the little one will be better for some fresh stuff about her. Get her a bright, sensible girl as a nurse; one who won't go rubbing her with calf's-foot jelly as Norah does; wasting good stuff outside that ought to go in, but will follow doctors' directions; which, as you must see pretty clearly by this time, Norah won't; because they give the poor little wench pain. Now, I'm not above being nesh for other folks myself. I can stand a good blow, and never change colour; but, set me in the operating room in the infirmary, and I turn as sick as a girl. Yet, if need were, I would hold the little wench on my knees while she screeched with pain, if it were to do her poor back good. Nay, nay, wench! keep your white looks for the time when it comes I don't say it ever will. But this I know, Norah will spare the child and cheat the doctor, if she can. Now, I say, give the bairn a year or two's chance, and then, when the pack of doctors have done their best and, maybe, the old lady has gone we'll have Norah back or do better for her.'

The pack of doctors could do no good to little Ailsie. She was beyond their power. But her father (for so he insisted on being called, and also on Alice's no longer retaining the appellation of Mamma, but becoming henceforward Mother), by his healthy cheerfulness of manner, his clear decision of purpose, his odd turns and quirks of humour, added to his real strong love for the helpless little girl, infused a new element of brightness and confidence into her life; and, though her back remained the same, her general health was strengthened, and Alice, never going beyond a smile herself, had the pleasure of seeing her child taught to laugh.

As for Alice's own life, it was happier than it had ever been before. Mr Openshaw required no demonstration, no expressions of affection from her. Indeed, these would rather have disgusted him. Alice could love deeply, but could not talk about it. The perpetual requirement of loving words, looks, and caresses, and misconstruing their absence into absence of love, had been the great trial of her former married life. Now, all went on clear and straight, under the guidance of her husband's strong sense, warm heart, and powerful will. Year by year their worldly prosperity increased. At Mrs Wilson's death, Norah came back to them as nurse to the newly-born little Edwin; into which post she was not installed without a pretty strong oration on the part of the proud and happy father, who declared that if he found out that Norah ever tried to screen the boy by a falsehood, or to make him nesh either in body or mind, she should go that very day. Norah and Mr Openshaw were not on the most thoroughly cordial terms; neither of them fully recognizing or appreciating the other's best qualities.

This was the previous history of the Lancashire family who had now removed to London.

They had been there about a year, when Mr Openshaw suddenly informed his wife that he had determined to heal long-standing feuds, and had asked his uncle and aunt Chadwick to come and pay them a visit and see London. Mrs Openshaw had never seen this uncle and aunt of her husband's. Years before she had married him, there had been a quarrel. All she knew was, that Mr Chadwick was a small manufacturer in a country town in South Lancashire. She was extremely pleased that the breach was to be healed, and began making preparations to render their visit pleasant.

They arrived at last. Going to see London was such an event to them, that Mrs Chadwick had made all new linen fresh for the occasion, from night-caps downwards; and as for gowns, ribbons, and collars, she might have been going into the wilds of Canada where never a shop is, so large was her stock. A fortnight before the day of her departure for London, she had formally called to take leave of all her acquaintance; saying she should need every bit of the intermediate time for packing up. It was like a second wedding in her imagination; and, to complete the resemblance which an entirely new wardrobe made between the two events, her husband brought her back from Manchester, on the last market-day before they set off, a gorgeous pearl and amethyst brooch, saying, 'Lunnon should see that Lancashire folks knew a handsome thing when they saw it.'

For some time after Mr and Mrs Chadwick arrived at the Openshaws' there was no opportunity for wearing this brooch; but at length they obtained an order to see Buckingham Palace, and the spirit of loyalty demanded that Mrs Chadwick should wear her best clothes in visiting the abode of her sovereign. On her return she hastily changed her dress; for Mr Openshaw had planned that they should go to Richmond, drink tea, and return by moonlight. Accordingly, about five o'clock, Mr and Mrs Openshaw and Mr and Mrs Chadwick set off.

The housemaid and cook sat below, Norah hardly knew where. She was always engrossed in the nursery in tending her two children, and in sitting by the restless, excitable Ailsie till she fell asleep. By and by the housemaid Bessy tapped gently at the door. Norah went to her, and they spoke in whispers.

'Nurse! there's someone downstairs wants you.'

'Wants me! who is it?'

'A gentleman'

'A gentleman? Nonsense!'

'Well! a man, then, and he asks for you, and he rang at the front-door bell, and has walked into the dining-room.'

'You should never have let him,' exclaimed Norah. 'Master and missus out'

'I did not want him to come in; but, when he heard you lived here, he walked past me, and sat down on the first chair, and said, "Tell her to come and speak to me." There is no gas lighted in the room, and supper is all set out.'

'He'll be off with the spoons!' exclaimed Norah, putting the housemaid's fear into words, and preparing to leave the room; first, however, giving a look to Ailsie, sleeping soundly and calmly.

Downstairs she went, uneasy fears stirring in her bosom. Before she entered the dining-room she provided herself with a candle, and, with it in her hand, she went in, looking around her in the darkness for her visitor.

He was standing up, holding by the table. Norah and he looked at each other; gradual recognition coming into their eyes.

'Norah?' at length he asked.

'Who are you?' asked Norah, with the sharp tones of alarm and incredulity. 'I don't know you'; trying, by futile words of disbelief, to do away with the terrible fact before her.

'Am I so changed?' he said pathetically. 'I dare say I am. But, Norah, tell me!' he breathed hard, 'where is my wife? Is she, is she alive?'

He came nearer to Norah, and would have taken her hand; but she backed away from him; looking at him all the time with staring eyes, as if he were some horrible object. Yet he was a handsome, bronzed, good-looking fellow, with beard and moustache, giving him a foreign-looking aspect; but his eyes! there was no mistaking those eager, beautiful eyes the very same that Norah had watched not half an hour ago, till sleep stole softly over them.

'Tell me, Norah, I can bear it - I have feared it so often. Is she dead?' Norah still kept silence. 'She is dead!' He hung on Norah's words and looks, as if for confirmation or contradiction.

'What shall I do?' groaned Norah. 'Oh, sir! why did you come? how did you find me out? where have you been? We thought you dead, we did indeed!' She poured out words and questions to gain time, as if time would help her.

'Norah! answer me this question straight, by yes or no. Is my wife dead?'

'No, she is not,' said Norah, slowly and heavily.

'Oh, what a relief! Did she receive my letters? But perhaps you don't know. Why did you leave her? Where is she? Oh, Norah, tell me all quickly!'

'Mr Frank!' said Norah at last, almost driven to bay by her terror lest her mistress should return at any moment and find him there, unable to consider what was best to be done or said, rushing at something decisive, because she could not endure her present state: 'Mr Frank! we never heard a line from you, and the shipowners said you had gone down, you and everyone else. We thought you were dead, if ever man was, and poor Miss Alice and her little sick, helpless child! Oh, sir, you must guess it,' cried the poor creature at last, bursting out into a passionate fit of crying, 'for indeed I cannot tell it. But it was no one's fault. God help us all this night!'

Norah had sat down. She trembled too much to stand. He took her hands in his. He squeezed them hard, as if, by physical pressure, the truth could be wrung out.

'Norah.' This time his tone was calm, stagnant as despair. 'She has married again!'

Norah shook her head sadly. The grasp slowly relaxed. The man had fainted.

There was brandy in the room. Norah forced some drops into Mr Frank's mouth, chafed his hands, and when mere animal life returned, before the mind poured in its flood of memories and thoughts she lifted him up, and rested his head against her knees. Then she put a few crumbs of bread taken from the supper-table, soaked in brandy, into his mouth. Suddenly he sprang to his feet.

'Where is she? Tell me this instant.' He looked so wild, so mad, so desperate, that Norah felt herself to be in bodily danger; but her time of dread had gone by. She had been afraid to tell him the truth, and then she had been a coward. Now, her wits were sharpened by the sense of his desperate state. He must leave the house. She would pity him afterwards; but now she must rather command and upbraid; for he must leave the house before her mistress came home. That one necessity stood clear before her.

'She is not here: that is enough for you to know. Nor can I say exactly where she is' (which was true to the letter if not to the spirit). 'Go away, and tell me where to find you tomorrow, and I will tell you all. My master and mistress may come back at any minute, and then what would become of me, with a strange man in the house?'

Such an argument was too petty to touch his excited mind.

'I don't care for your master and mistress. If your master is a man, he must feel for me, poor shipwrecked sailor that I am, kept for years a prisoner amongst savages, always, always, always thinking of my wife and my home, dreaming of her by night, talking to her though she could not hear, by day. I loved her more than all heaven and earth put together. Tell me where she is, this instant, you wretched woman, who salved over her wickedness to her, as you do to me!'

The clock struck ten. Desperate positions require desperate measures.

'If you will leave the house now, I will come to you tomorrow and tell you all. What is more, you shall see your child now. She lies sleeping upstairs. Oh, sir, you have a child, you do not know that as yet, a little weakly girl with just a heart and soul beyond her years. We have reared her up with such care! We watched her, for we thought for many a year she might die any day, and we tended her, and no hard thing has come near her, and no rough word has ever been said to her. And now you come and will take her life into your hand, and will crush it. Strangers to her have been kind to her; but her own father--Mr Frank, I am her nurse, and I love her, and I tend her, and I would do anything for her that I could. Her mother's heart beats as hers beats; and, if she suffers a pain, her mother trembles all over. If she is happy, it is her mother that smiles and is glad. If she is growing stronger, her mother is healthy: if she dwindles, her mother languishes. If she dies well, I don't know; it is not everyone can lie down and die when they wish it. Come upstairs, Mr Frank, and see your child. Seeing her will do good to your poor heart. Then go away, in God's name, just this one night; tomorrow, if need be, you can do anything, kill us all if you will, or show yourself a great, grand man, whom God will bless for ever and ever. Come, Mr Frank, the look of a sleeping child is sure to give peace.'

She led him upstairs; at first almost helping his steps, till they came near the nursery door. She had well nigh forgotten the existence of little Edwin. It struck upon her with affright as the shaded light fell over the other cot; but she skilfully threw that corner of the room into darkness, and let the light fall on the sleeping Ailsie. The child had thrown down the coverings, and her deformity, as she lay with her back to them, was plainly visible through her slight nightgown. Her little face, deprived of the lustre of her eyes, looked wan and pinched, and had a pathetic expression in it, even as she slept. The poor father looked and looked with hungry, wistful eyes, into which the big tears came swelling up slowly and dropped heavily down, as he stood trembling and shaking all over. Norah was angry with herself for growing impatient of the length of time that long lingering gaze lasted. She thought that she waited for full half an hour before Frank stirred. And then instead of going away he sank down on his knees by the bedside, and buried his face in the clothes. Little Ailsie stirred uneasily. Norah pulled him up in terror. She could afford no more time, even for prayer, in her extremity of fear; for surely the next moment would bring her mistress home. She took him forcibly by the arm; but, as he was going, his eye lighted on the other bed; he stopped. Intelligence came back into his face. His hands clenched.

'His child?' he asked.

'Her child,' replied Norah. 'God watches over him,' she said instinctively; for Frank's looks excited her fears, and she needed to remind herself of the Protector of the helpless. 'God has not watched over me,' he said, in despair; his thoughts apparently recoiling on his own desolate, deserted state. But Norah had no time for pity. Tomorrow she would be as compassionate as her heart prompted. At length she guided him downstairs, and shut the outer door, and bolted it as if by bolts to keep out facts.

Then she went back into the dining-room, and effaced all traces of his presence, as far as she could. She went upstairs to the nursery and sat there, her head on her hand, thinking what was to come of all this misery. It seemed to her very long before her master and mistress returned; yet it was hardly eleven o'clock. She heard the loud, hearty Lancashire voices on the stairs; and, for the first time, she understood the contrast of the desolation of the poor man who had so lately gone forth in lonely despair.

It almost put her out of patience to see Mrs Openshaw come in, calmly smiling, handsomely dressed, happy, easy, to inquire after her children.

'Did Ailsie go to sleep comfortably?' she whispered to Norah.

'Yes.'

Her mother bent over her, looking at her slumbers with the soft eyes of love. How little she dreamed who had looked on her last! Then she went to Edwin, with perhaps less wistful anxiety in her countenance, but more of pride. She took off her things, to go down to supper. Norah saw her no more that night.

Beside having a door into the passage, the sleeping-nursery opened out of Mr and Mrs Openshaw's room, in order that they might have the children more immediately under their own eyes. Early the next summer's morning, Mrs Openshaw was awakened by Ailsie's startled call of 'Mother! mother!' She sprang up, put on her dressing-gown, and went to her child. Ailsie was only half awake, and in a not unusual state of terror.

'Who was he, mother? Tell me!'

'Who, my darling? No one is here. You have been dreaming, love. Waken up quite. See, it is broad daylight.'

'Yes,' said Ailsie, looking round her; then clinging to her mother, 'but a man was here in the night, mother.'

'Nonsense, little goose. No man has ever come near you!'

'Yes, he did. He stood there. Just by Norah. A man with hair and a beard. And he knelt down and said his prayers. Norah knows he was here, mother' (half angrily, as Mrs Openshaw shook her head in smiling incredulity).

'Well! we will ask Norah when she comes,' said Mrs Openshaw, soothingly. 'But we won't talk any more about him now. It is not five o'clock; it is too early for you to get up. Shall I fetch you a book and read to you?'

'Don't leave me, mother,' said the child, clinging to her. So Mrs Openshaw sat on the bedside talking to Ailsie, and telling her of what they had done at Richmond the evening before, until the little girl's eyes slowly closed and she once more fell asleep.

'What was the matter?' asked Mr Openshaw, as his wife returned to bed.

'Ailsie wakened up in a fright, with some story of a man having been in the room to say his prayers, a dream, I suppose.' And no more was said at the time.

Mrs Openshaw had almost forgotten the whole affair when she got up about seven o'clock. But, by and by, she heard a sharp altercation going on in the nursery, Norah speaking angrily to Ailsie, a most unusual thing. Both Mr and Mrs Openshaw listened in astonishment.

'Hold your tongue, Ailsie! let me hear none of your dreams; never let me hear you tell that story again!'

Ailsie began to cry.

Mr Openshaw opened the door of communication, before his wife could say a word. 'Norah, come here!'

The nurse stood at the door, defiant. She perceived she had been heard, but she was desperate.

'Don't let me hear you speak in that manner to Ailsie again,' he said sternly, and shut the door.

Norah was infinitely relieved; for she had dreaded some questioning; and a little blame for sharp speaking was what she could well bear, if cross-examination was let alone. Downstairs they went, Mr Openshaw carrying Ailsie; the sturdy Edwin coming step by step, right foot foremost, always holding his mother's hand. Each child was placed in a chair by the breakfast-table, and then Mr and Mrs Openshaw stood together at the window, awaiting their visitors' appearance and making plans for the day. There was a pause. Suddenly Mr Openshaw turned to Ailsie, and said:

'What a little goosy somebody is with her dreams, wakening up poor, tired mother in the middle of the night, with a story of a man being in the room.'

'Father! I'm sure I saw him,' said Ailsie, half-crying. 'I don't want to make Norah angry; but I was not asleep, for all she says I was. I had been asleep and I wakened up quite wide awake, though I was so frightened. I kept my eyes nearly shut, and I saw the man quite plain. A great brown man with a beard. He said his prayers. And then looked at Edwin. And then Norah took him by the arm and led him away, after they had whispered a bit together.'

'Now, my little woman must be reasonable,' said Mr Openshaw, who was always patient with Ailsie. 'There was no man in the house last night at all. No man comes into the house, as you know, if you think; much less goes up into the nursery. But sometimes we dream something has happened, and the dream is so like reality, that you are not the first person, little woman, who has stood out that the thing has really happened.'

'But, indeed, it was not a dream!' said Ailsie, beginning to cry.

Just then Mr and Mrs Chadwick came down, looking grave and discomposed. All during breakfast-time they were silent and uncomfortable. As soon as the breakfast things were taken away, and the children had been carried upstairs, Mr Chadwick began, in an evidently preconcerted manner, to inquire if his nephew was certain that all his servants were honest; for, that Mrs Chadwick had that morning missed a very valuable brooch, which she had worn the day before. She remembered taking it off when she came home from Buckingham Palace. Mr Openshaw's face contracted into hard lines; grew like what it was before he had known his wife and her child. He rang the bell, even before his uncle had done speaking. It was answered by the housemaid.

'Mary, was anyone here last night, while we were away?'

'A man, sir, came to speak to Norah.'

'To speak to Norah! Who was he? How long did he stay?'

'I'm sure I can't tell, sir. He came, perhaps about nine. I went up to tell Norah in the nursery, and she came down to speak to him. She let him out, sir. She will know who he was, and how long he stayed.'

She waited a moment to be asked any more questions, but she was not, so she went away. A minute afterwards Mr Openshaw made as though he were going out of the room; but his wife laid her hand on his arm.

'Do not speak to her before the children,' she said, in her low, quiet voice. 'I will go up and question her.'

'No! I must speak to her. You must know,' said he, turning to his uncle and aunt, 'my missus has an old servant, as faithful as ever woman was, I do believe, as far as love goes, but at the same time, who does not speak truth, as even the missus must allow. Now, my notion is, that this Norah of ours has been come over by some good-for-nothing chap (for she's at the time o' life when they say women pray for husbands "any, good Lord, any") and has let him into our house, and the chap has made off with your brooch, and m'appen many another thing beside. It's only saying that Norah is soft-hearted and doesn't stick at a white lie, that's all, missus.'

It was curious to notice how his tone, his eyes, his whole face was changed, as he spoke to his wife; but he was the resolute man through all. She knew better than to oppose him; so she went upstairs, and told Norah that her master wanted to speak to her, and that she would take care of the children in the meanwhile.

Norah rose to go, without a word. Her thoughts were these:

'If they tear me to pieces, they shall never know through me. He may come and then, just Lord have mercy upon us all! for some of us are dead folk to a certainty. But he shall do it; not me.'

You may fancy, now, her look of determination, as she faced her master alone in the dining-room; Mr and Mrs Chadwick having left the affair in their nephew's hands, seeing that he took it up with such vehemence.

'Norah! Who was that man that came to my house last night?'

'Man, sir!' As if infinitely surprised; but it was only to gain time.

'Yes; the man that Mary let in; that she went upstairs to the nursery to tell you about; that you came down to speak to; the same chap, I make no doubt, that you took into the nursery to have your talk out with; the one Ailsie saw, and afterwards dreamed about; thinking, poor wench! she saw him say his prayers, when nothing, I'll be bound, was further from his thoughts; the one that took Mrs Chadwick's brooch, value ten pounds. Now, Norah! Don't go off. I'm as sure as my name's Thomas Openshaw that you knew nothing of this robbery. But I do think you've been imposed on, and that's the truth. Some good-for-nothing chap has been making up to you, and you've been just like all other women, and have turned a soft place in your heart to him; and he came last night a-lovyering, and you had him up in the nursery, and he made use of his opportunities, and made off with a few things on his way down! Come, now, Norah; it's no blame to you, only you must not be such a fool again! Tell us,' he continued, 'what name he gave you, Norah. I'll be bound, it was not the right one; but it will be a clue for the police.'

Norah drew herself up. 'You may ask that question, and taunt me with my being single, and with my credulity, as you will, Master Openshaw. You'll get no answer from me. As for the brooch, and the story of theft and burglary; if any friend ever came to see me (which I defy you to prove, and deny), he'd be just as much above doing such a thing as you yourself, Mr Openshaw and more so, too; for I'm not at all sure as everything you have is rightly come by, or would be yours long, if every man had his own.' She meant, of course, his wife; but he understood her to refer to his property in goods and chattels. 'Now, my good woman,' said he, 'I'll just tell you truly, I never trusted you out and out; but my wife liked you, and I thought you had many a good point about you. If you once begin to sauce me, I'll have the police to you, and get out the truth in a court of justice, if you'll not tell it me quietly and civilly here. Now, the best thing you can do is quietly to tell me who the fellow is. Look here! a man comes to my house; asks for you; you take him upstairs; a valuable brooch is missing next day; we know that you, and Mary, and cook, are honest; but you refuse to tell us who the man is. Indeed, you've told me one lie already about him, saying no one was here last night. Now, I just put it to you, what do you think a policeman would say to this, or a magistrate? A magistrate would soon make you tell the truth, my good woman.'

'There's never the creature born that should get it out of me,' said Norah. 'Not unless I choose to tell.'

'I've a great mind to see,' said Mr Openshaw, growing angry at the defiance. Then, checking himself, he thought before he spoke again:

'Norah, for your missus' sake I don't want to go to extremities. Be a sensible woman, if you can. It's no great disgrace, after all, to have been taken in. I ask you once more, as a friend, who was this man that you let into my house last night?'

No answer. He repeated the question in an impatient tone. Still no answer. Norah's lips were set in determination not to speak.

'Then there is but one thing to be done. I shall send for a policeman.'

'You will not,' said Norah, starting forward. 'You shall not, sir! No policeman shall touch me. I know nothing of the brooch, but I know this: ever since I was four-and-twenty, I have thought more of your wife than of myself: ever since I saw her, a poor motherless girl, put upon in her uncle's house, I have thought more of serving her than of serving myself! I have cared for her and her child, as nobody ever cared for me. I don't cast blame on you, sir, but I say it's ill giving up one's life to anyone; for, at the end, they will turn round upon you, and forsake you. Why does not my missus come herself to suspect me? Maybe, she is gone for the police? But I don't stay here, either for police, or magistrate, or master. You're an unlucky lot. I believe there's a curse on you. I'll leave you this very day. Yes! I'll leave that poor Ailsie, too. I will! No good ever will come to you!'

Mr Openshaw was utterly astonished at this speech; most of which was completely unintelligible to him, as may easily be supposed. Before he could make up his mind what to say, or what to do, Norah had left the room. I do not think he had ever really intended to send for the police to this old servant of his wife's; for he had never for a moment doubted her perfect honesty. But he had intended to compel her to tell him who the man was, and in this he was baffled. He was, consequently, much irritated. He returned to his uncle and aunt in a state of great annoyance and perplexity, and told them he could get nothing out of the woman; that some man had been in the house the night before; but that she refused to tell who he was. At this moment his wife came in, greatly agitated, and asked what had happened to Norah; for that she had put on her things in passionate haste, and left the house.

'This looks suspicious,' said Mr Chadwick. 'It is not the way in which an honest person would have acted.'

Mr Openshaw kept silence. He was sorely perplexed. But Mrs Openshaw turned round on Mr Chadwick, with a sudden fierceness no one ever saw in her before.

'You don't know Norah, uncle! She is gone because she is deeply hurt at being suspected. Oh, I wish I had seen her, that I had spoken to her myself. She would have told me anything.' Alice wrung her hands.

'I must confess,' continued Mr Chadwick to his nephew, in a lower voice, 'I can't make you out. You used to be a word and a blow, and oftenest the blow first; and now, when there is every cause for suspicion, you just do nought. Your missus is a very good woman, I grant; but she may have been put upon as well as other folk, I suppose. If you don't send for the police, I shall.'

'Very well,' replied Mr Openshaw, surlily. 'I can't clear Norah. She won't clear herself, as I believe she might if she would. Only I wash my hands of it; for I am sure the woman herself is honest, and she's lived a long time with my wife, and I don't like her to come to shame.'

'But she will then be forced to clear herself. That, at any rate, will be a good thing.'

'Very well, very well! I am heart-sick of the whole business. Come, Alice, come up to the babies; they'll be in a sore way. I tell you, uncle,' he said, turning round once more to Mr Chadwick, suddenly and sharply, after his eye had fallen on Alice's wan, tearful, anxious face, 'I'll have no sending for the police, after all. I'll buy my aunt twice as handsome a brooch this very day; but I'll not have Norah suspected, and my missus plagued. There's for you!'

He and his wife left the room. Mr Chadwick quietly waited till he was out of hearing, and then said to his wife, 'For all Tom's heroics, I'm just quietly going for a detective, wench. Thou need'st know nought about it.'

He went to the police-station and made a statement of the case. He was gratified by the impression which the evidence against Norah seemed to make. The men all agreed in his opinion, and steps were to be immediately taken to find out where she was. Most probably, as they suggested, she had gone at once to the man, who, to all appearance, was her lover. When Mr Chadwick asked how they would find her out, they smiled, shook their heads, and spoke of mysterious but infallible ways and means. He returned to his nephew's house with a very comfortable opinion of his own sagacity. He was met by his wife with a penitent face.

'Oh, master, I've found my brooch! It was just sticking by its pin in the flounce of my brown silk, that I wore yesterday. I took it off in a hurry, and it must have caught in it; and I hung up my gown in the closet. Just now, when I was going to fold it up, there was the brooch! I am very vexed, but I never dreamt but what it was lost!'

Her husband, muttering something very like 'Confound thee and thy brooch too! I wish I'd never given it thee,' snatched up his hat, and rushed back to the station, hoping to be in time to stop the police from searching for Norah. But a detective was already gone off on the errand.

Where was Norah? Half mad with the strain of the fearful secret, she had hardly slept through the night for thinking what must be done. Upon this terrible state of mind had come Ailsie's questions, showing that she had seen the Man, as the unconscious child called her father. Lastly came the suspicion of her honesty. She was little less than crazy as she ran upstairs and dashed on her bonnet and shawl; leaving all else, even her purse, behind her. In that house she would not stay. That was all she knew or was clear about. She would not even see the children again, for fear it should weaken her. She dreaded above everything Mr Frank's return to claim his wife. She could not tell what remedy there was for a sorrow so tremendous, for her to stay to witness. The desire of escaping from the coming event was a stronger motive for her departure, than her soreness about the suspicions directed against her; although this last had been the final goad to the course she took. She walked a way almost at headlong speed; sobbing as she went, as she had not dared to do during the past night for fear of exciting wonder in those who might hear her. Then she stopped. An idea came into her mind that she would leave London altogether, and betake herself to her native town of Liverpool. She felt in her pocket for her purse as she drew near the Euston Square station with this intention. She had left it at home. Her poor head aching, her eyes swollen with crying, she had to stand still, and think, as well as she could, where next she should bend her steps. Suddenly the thought flashed into her mind that she would go and find out poor Mr Frank. She had been hardly kind to him the night before, though her heart had bled for him ever since. She remembered his telling her, when she inquired for his address, almost as she had pushed him out of the door, of some hotel in a street not far distant from Euston Square. Thither she went: with what intention she scarcely knew, but to assuage her conscience by telling him how much she pitied him. In her present state she felt herself unfit to counsel, or restrain, or assist, or do aught else but sympathize and weep. The people of the inn said such a person had been there; had arrived only the day before; had gone out soon after arrival, leaving his luggage in their care; but had never come back. Norah asked for leave to sit down, and await the gentleman's return. The landlady, pretty secure in the deposit of luggage against any probable injury showed her into a room, and quietly locked the door on the outside. Norah was utterly worn out, and fell asleep - a shivering, starting, uneasy slumber, which lasted for hours.

The detective, meanwhile, had come up with her some time before she entered the hotel, into which he followed her. Asking the landlady to detain her for an hour or so, without giving any reason beyond showing his authority (which made the landlady applaud herself a good deal for having locked her in), he went back to the police-station to report his proceedings. He could have taken her directly; but his object was, if possible, to trace out the man who was supposed to have committed the robbery. Then he heard of the discovery of the brooch; and consequently did not care to return.

Norah slept till even the summer evening began to close in, Then started up. Someone was at the door. It would be Mr Frank; and she dizzily pushed back her ruffled grey hair which had fallen over her eyes, and stood looking to see him. Instead, there came in Mr Openshaw and a policeman.

'This is Norah Kennedy,' said Mr Openshaw.

'Oh, sir,' said Norah, 'I did not touch the brooch; indeed I did not. Oh, sir, I cannot live to be thought so badly of'; and very sick and faint, she suddenly sank down on the ground. To her surprise, Mr Openshaw raised her up very tenderly. Even the policeman helped to lay her on the sofa; and, at Mr Openshaw's desire, he went for some wine and sandwiches; for the poor gaunt woman lay there almost as if dead with weariness and exhaustion.

'Norah,' said Mr Openshaw, in his kindest voice, 'the brooch is found. It was hanging to Mrs Chadwick's gown. I beg your pardon. Most truly I beg your pardon, for having troubled you about it. My wife is almost broken-hearted. Eat, Norah or, stay, first drink this glass of wine,' said he, lifting her head, and pouring a little down her throat.

As she drank, she remembered where she was, and who she was waiting for. She suddenly pushed Mr Openshaw away, saying, 'Oh, sir, you must go. You must not stop a minute. If he comes back, he will kill you.'

'Alas, Norah! I do not know who "he" is. But someone is gone away who will never come back: someone who knew you, and whom I am afraid you cared for.'

'I don't understand you, sir,' said Norah, her master's kind and sorrowful manner bewildering her yet more than his words. The policeman had left the room at Mr Openshaw's desire, and they two were alone.

'You know what I mean, when I say someone is gone who will never come back. I mean that he is dead!'

'Who?' said Norah, trembling all over.

'A poor man has been found in the Thames this morning drowned.'

'Did he drown himself?' asked Norah, solemnly.

'God only knows,' replied Mr Openshaw, in the same tone. 'Your name and address at our house were found in his pocket; that, and his purse, were the only things that were found upon him. I am sorry to say it, my poor Norah; but you are required to go and identify him.'

'To what?' asked Norah.

'To say who it is. It is always done, in order that some reason may be discovered for the suicide, if suicide it was. I make no doubt, he was the man who came to see you at our house last night. It is very sad, I know.' He made pauses between each little clause, in order to try and bring back her senses, which he feared were wandering so wild and sad was her look.

'Master Openshaw,' said she, at last, 'I've a dreadful secret to tell you, only you must never breathe it to anyone, and you and I must hide it away for ever. I thought to have done it all by myself, but I see I cannot. Yon poor man yes! the dead, drowned creature is, I fear, Mr Frank, my mistress's first husband!'

Mr Openshaw sat down, as if shot. He did not speak; but, after a while, he signed to Norah to go on.

'He came to me the other night, when, God be thanked! you were all away at Richmond. He asked me if his wife was dead or alive. I was a brute, and thought more of your all coming home than of his sore trial; I spoke out sharp, and said she was married again, and very content and happy. I all but turned him away: and now he lies dead and cold.' 'God forgive me!' said Mr Openshaw.

'God forgive us all!' said Norah. 'Yon poor man needs forgiveness, perhaps, less than any one among us. He had been among the savages – shipwrecked - I know not what and he had written letters which had never reached my poor missus.'

'He saw his child!'

'He saw her - yes! I took him up, to give his thoughts another start; for I believed he was going mad on my hands. I came to seek him here, as I more than half promised. My mind misgave me when I heard he never came in. Oh, sir, it must be him!'

Mr Openshaw rang the bell. Norah was almost too much stunned to wonder at what he did. He asked for writing materials, wrote a letter, and then said to Norah:

'I am writing to Alice, to say I shall be unavoidably absent for a few days; that I have found you; that you are well, and send her your love, and will come home tomorrow. You must go with me to the police court; you must identify the body; I will pay high to keep names and details out of the papers.'

'But where are you going, sir?'

He did not answer her directly. Then he said:

'Norah! I must go with you, and look on the face of the man whom I have so injured - unwittingly, it is true; but it seems to me as if I had killed him. I will lay his head in the grave as if he were my only brother: and how he must have hated me! I cannot go home to my wife till all that I can do for him is done. Then I go with a dreadful secret on my mind. I shall never speak of it again, after these days are over. I know you will not, either.' He shook hands with her; and they never named the subject again, the one to the other.

Norah went home to Alice the next day. Not a word was said on the cause of her abrupt departure a day or two before. Alice had been charged by her husband, in his letter, not to allude to the supposed theft of the brooch; so she, implicitly obedient to those whom she loved both by nature and habit, was entirely silent on the subject, only treated Norah with the most tender respect, as if to make up for unjust suspicion.

Nor did Alice inquire into the reason why Mr Openshaw had been absent during his uncle and aunt's visit, after he had once said that it was unavoidable. He came back grave and quiet; and from that time forth was curiously changed. More thoughtful, and perhaps less active; quite as decided in conduct, but with new and different rules for the guidance of that conduct. Towards Alice he could hardly be more kind than he had always been; but he now seemed to look upon her as someone sacred, and to be treated with reverence, as well as tenderness. He throve in business, and made a large fortune, one half of which was settled upon her.

Long years after these events, a few months after her mother died, Ailsie and her 'father' (as she always called Mr Openshaw) drove to a cemetery a little way out of town, and she was carried to a certain mound by her maid, who was then sent back to the carriage. There was a headstone, with F.W. and a date upon it. That was all. Sitting by the grave, Mr Openshaw told her the story; and for the sad fate of that poor father whom she had never seen, he shed the only tears she ever saw fall from his eyes.

The Half Brothers

My mother was twice married. She never spoke of her first husband, and it is only from other people that I have learnt what little I know about him. I believe she was scarcely seventeen when she was married to him: and he was barely one-and-twenty. He rented a small farm up in Cumberland, somewhere towards the sea-coast; but he was perhaps too young and inexperienced to have the charge of land and cattle: anyhow, his affairs did not prosper, and he fell into ill health, and died of consumption before they had been three years man and wife, leaving my mother a young widow of twenty, with a little child only just able to walk, and the farm on her hands for four years more by the lease, with half the stock on it dead, or sold off one by one to pay the more pressing debts, and with no money to purchase more, or even to buy the provisions needed for the small consumption of every day. There was another child coming, too; and sad and sorry, I believe, she was to think of it. A dreary winter she must have had in her lonesome dwelling, with never another near it for miles around; her sister came to bear her company, and they two planned and plotted how to make every penny they could raise go as far as possible. I can't tell you how it happened that my little sister, whom I never saw, came to sicken and die; but, as if my poor mother's cup was not full enough, only a fortnight before Gregory was born the little girl took ill of scarlet fever, and in a week she lay dead. My mother was, I believe, just stunned with this last blow. My aunt has told me that she did not cry; aunt Fanny would have been thankful if she had; but she sat holding the poor wee lassie's hand and looking in her pretty, pale, dead face, without so much as shedding a tear. And it was all the same, when they had to take her away to be buried. She just kissed the child, and sat her down in the window-seat to watch the little black train of people (neighbours, my aunt, and one far-off cousin, who were all the friends they could muster) go winding away amongst the snow, which had fallen thinly over the country the night before. When my aunt came back from the funeral, she found my mother in the same place, and as dry-eyed as ever. So she continued until after Gregory was born; and, somehow, his coming seemed to loosen the tears, and she cried day and night, till my aunt and the other watcher looked at each other in dismay, and would fain have stopped her if they had but known how. But she bade them let her alone, and not be over-anxious, for every drop she shed eased her brain, which had been in a terrible state before for want of the power to cry. She seemed after that to think of nothing but her new little baby; she had hardly appeared to remember either her husband or her little daughter that lay dead in Brigham churchyard, at least so aunt Fanny said, but she was a great talker, and my mother was very silent by nature, and I think aunt Fanny may have been mistaken in believing that my mother never thought of her husband and child just because she never spoke about them. Aunt Fanny was older than my mother, and had a way of treating her like a child; but, for all that, she was a kind, warm-hearted creature, who thought more of her sister's welfare than she did of her own and it was on her bit of money that they principally lived, and on what the two could earn by working for the great Glasgow sewing-merchants. But by-and-by my mother's eye-sight began to fail. It was not that she was exactly blind, for she could see well enough to guide herself about the house, and to do a good deal of domestic work; but she could no longer do fine sewing and earn money. It must have been with the heavy crying she had had in her day, for she was but a young creature at this time, and as pretty a young woman, I have heard people say, as any on the country side. She took it sadly to heart that she could no longer gain anything towards the keep of herself and her child. My aunt Fanny would fain have persuaded her that she had enough to do in managing their cottage and minding Gregory; but my mother knew that they were pinched, and that aunt Fanny herself had not as much to eat, even of the commonest kind of food, as she could have done with; and as for Gregory, he was not a strong lad, and needed, not more food - for he always had enough, whoever went short but better nourishment, and more flesh-meat. One day, it was aunt Fanny who told me all this about my poor mother, long after her death, as the sisters were sitting together, aunt Fanny working, and my mother hushing Gregory to sleep, William Preston, who was afterwards my father, came in. He was reckoned an old bachelor; I suppose he was long past forty, and he was one of the wealthiest farmers thereabouts, and had known my grandfather well, and my mother and my aunt in their more prosperous days. He sat down, and began to twirl his hat by way of being agreeable; my aunt Fanny talked, and he listened and looked at my mother. But he said very little, either on that visit, or on many another that he paid before he spoke out what had been the real purpose of his calling so often all along, and from the very first time he came to their house. One Sunday, however, my aunt Fanny stayed away from church, and took care of the child, and my mother went alone. When she came back, she ran straight upstairs, without going into the kitchen to look at Gregory or speak any word to her sister, and aunt Fanny heard her cry as if her heart was breaking; so she went up and scolded her right well through the bolted door, till at last she got her to open it. And then she threw herself on my aunt's neck, and told her that William Preston had asked her to marry him, and had promised to take good charge of her boy, and to let him want for nothing, neither in the way of keep nor of education, and that she had consented. Aunt Fanny was a good deal shocked at this; for, as I have said, she had often thought that my mother had forgotten her first husband very quickly, and now here was proof positive of it, if she could so soon think of marrying again. Besides as aunt Fanny used to say, she herself would have been a far more suitable match for a man of William Preston's age than Helen, who, though she was a widow, had not seen her four-and-twentieth summer. However, as aunt Fanny said, they had not asked her advice; and there was much to be said on the other side of the question. Helen's eyesight would never be good for much again, and as William Preston's wife she would never need to do anything, if she chose to sit with her hands before her; and a boy was a great charge to a widowed mother; and now there would be a decent steady man to see after him. So, by-and-by, aunt Fanny seemed to take a brighter view of the marriage than did my mother herself, who hardly ever looked up, and never smiled after the day when she promised William Preston to be his wife. But much as she had loved Gregory before, she seemed to love him more now. She was continually talking to him when they were alone, though he was far too young to understand her moaning words, or give her any comfort, except by his caresses.

At last William Preston and she were wed; and she went to be mistress of a well-stocked house, not above half-an-hour's walk from where aunt Fanny lived. I believe she did all that she could to please my father; and a more dutiful wife, I have heard him himself say, could never have been. But she did not love him, and he soon found it out. She loved Gregory, and she did not love him. Perhaps, love would have come in time, if he had been patient enough to wait; but it just turned him sour to see how her eye brightened and her colour came at the sight of that little child, while for him who had given her so much, she had only gentle words as cold as ice. He got to taunt her with the difference in her manner, as if that would bring love: and he took a positive dislike to Gregory, he was so jealous of the ready love that always gushed out like a spring of fresh water when he came near. He wanted her to love him more, and perhaps that was all well and good; but he wanted her to love her child less, and that was an evil wish. One day, he gave way to his temper, and cursed and swore at Gregory, who had got into some mischief, as children will; my mother made some excuse for him; my father said it was hard enough to have to keep another man's child, without having it perpetually held up in its naughtiness by his wife, who ought to be always in the same mind that he was; and so from little they got to more; and the end of it was, that my mother took to her bed before her time, and I was born that very day. My father was glad, and proud, and sorry, all in a breath; glad and proud that a son was born to him; and sorry for his poor wife's state, and to think how his angry words had brought it on. But he was a man who liked better to be angry than sorry, so he soon found out that it was all Gregory's fault, and owed him an additional grudge for having hastened my birth. He had another grudge against him before long. My mother began to sink the day after I was born. My father sent to Carlisle for doctors, and would have coined his heart's blood into gold to save her, if that could have been; but it could not. My aunt Fanny used to say sometimes, that she thought that Helen did not wish to live, and so just let herself die away without trying to take hold on life; but when I questioned her, she owned that my mother did all the doctors bade her do, with the same sort of uncomplaining patience with which she had acted through life. One of her last requests was to have Gregory laid in her bed by my side, and then she made him take hold of my little hand. Her husband came in while she was looking at us so, and when he bent tenderly over her to ask her how she felt now, and seemed to gaze on us two little half-brothers, with a grave sort of kindness, she looked up in his face and smiled, almost her first smile at him; and such a sweet smile! as more besides aunt Fanny have said. In an hour she was dead. Aunt Fanny came to live with us. It was the best thing that could be done. My father would have been glad to return to his old mode of bachelor life, but what could he do with two little children? He needed a woman to take care of him, and who so fitting as his wife's elder sister? So she had the charge of me from my birth; and for a time I was weakly, as was but natural, and she was always beside me, night and day watching over me, and my father nearly as anxious as she. For his land had come down from father to son for more than three hundred years, and he would have cared for me merely as his flesh and blood that was to inherit the land after him. But he needed something to love, for all that, to most people, he was a stern, hard man, and he took to me as, I fancy, he had taken to no human being before, as he might have taken to my mother, if she had had no former life for him to be jealous of. I loved him back again right heartily. I loved all around me, I believe, for everybody was kind to me. After a time, I overcame my original weakness of constitution, and was just a bonny, strong- looking lad whom every passer-by noticed, when my father took me with him to the nearest town.

At home I was the darling of my aunt, the tenderly-beloved of my father, the pet and plaything of the old domestics, the "young master" of the farm-labourers, before whom I played many a lordly antic, assuming a sort of authority which sat oddly enough, I doubt not, on such a baby as I was.

Gregory was three years older than I. Aunt Fanny was always kind to him in deed and in action, but she did not often think about him, she had fallen so completely into the habit of being engrossed by me, from the fact of my having come into her charge as a delicate baby. My father never got over his grudging dislike to his stepson, who had so innocently wrestled with him for the possession of my mother's heart. I mistrust me, too, that my father always considered him as the cause of my mother's death and my early delicacy; and utterly unreasonable as this may seem, I believe my father rather cherished his feeling of alienation to my brother as a duty, than strove to repress it. Yet not for the world would my father have grudged him anything that money could purchase. That was, as it were, in the bond when he had wedded my mother. Gregory was lumpish and loutish, awkward and ungainly, marring whatever he meddled in, and many a hard word and sharp scolding did he get from the people about the farm, who hardly waited till my father's back was turned before they rated the stepson. I am ashamed, my heart is sore to think how I fell into the fashion of the family, and slighted my poor orphan step-brother. I don't think I ever scouted him, or was wilfully ill-natured to him; but the habit of being considered in all things, and being treated as something uncommon and superior, made me insolent in my prosperity, and I exacted more than Gregory was always willing to grant, and then, irritated, I sometimes repeated the disparaging words I had heard others use with regard to him, without fully understanding their meaning. Whether he did or not I cannot tell. I am afraid he did. He used to turn silent and quiet; sullen and sulky, my father thought it: stupid, aunt Fanny used to call it. But every one said he was stupid and dull, and this stupidity and dullness grew upon him. He would sit without speaking a word, sometimes, for hours; then my father would bid him rise and do some piece of work, maybe, about the farm. And he would take three or four tellings before he would go. When we were sent to school, it was all the same. He could never be made to remember his lessons; the school-master grew weary of scolding and flogging, and at last advised my father just to take him away, and set him to some farm-work that might not be above his comprehension. I think he was more gloomy and stupid than ever after this, yet he was not a cross lad; he was patient and good- natured, and would try to do a kind turn for any one, even if they had been scolding or cuffing him not a minute before. But very often his attempts at kindness ended in some mischief to the very people he was trying to serve, owing to his awkward, ungainly ways. I suppose I was a clever lad; at any rate, I always got plenty of praise; and was, as we called it, the cock of the school. The schoolmaster said I could learn anything I chose, but my father, who had no great learning himself, saw little use in much for me, and took me away betimes, and kept me with him about the farm. Gregory was made into a kind of shepherd, receiving his training under old Adam, who was nearly past his work. I think old Adam was almost the first person who had a good opinion of Gregory. He stood to it that my brother had good parts, though he did not rightly know how to bring them out; and, for knowing the bearings of the Fells, he said he had never seen a lad like him. My father would try to bring Adam round to speak of Gregory's faults and shortcomings; but, instead of that, he would praise him twice as much, as soon as he found out what was my father's object.

One winter-time, when I was about sixteen, and Gregory nineteen, I was sent by my father on an errand to a place about seven miles distant by the road, but only about four by the Fells. He bade me return by the road, whichever way I took in going, for the evenings closed in early, and were often thick and misty; besides which, old Adam, now paralytic and bedridden, foretold a downfall of snow before long. I soon got to my journey's end, and soon had done my business; earlier by an hour, I thought, than my father had expected, so I took the decision of the way by which I would return into my own hands, and set off back again over the Fells, just as the first shades of evening began to fall. It looked dark and gloomy enough; but everything was so still that I thought I should have plenty of time to get home before the snow came down. Off I set at a pretty quick pace. But night came on quicker. The right path was clear enough in the day-time, although at several points two or three exactly similar diverged from the same place; but when there was a good light, the traveller was guided by the sight of distant objects, a piece of rock, a fall in the ground which were quite invisible to me now. I plucked up a brave heart, however, and took what seemed to me the right road. It was wrong, nevertheless, and led me whither I knew not, but to some wild boggy moor where the solitude seemed painful, intense, as if never footfall of man had come thither to break the silence. I tried to shout, with the dimmest possible hope of being heard, rather to reassure myself by the sound of my own voice; but my voice came husky and short, and yet it dismayed me; it seemed so weird and strange, in that noiseless expanse of black darkness. Suddenly the air was filled thick with dusky flakes, my face and hands were wet with snow. It cut me off from the slightest knowledge of where I was, for I lost every idea of the direction from which I had come, so that I could not even retrace my steps; it hemmed me in, thicker, thicker, with a darkness that might be felt. The boggy soil on which I stood quaked under me if I remained long in one place, and yet I dared not move far. All my youthful hardiness seemed to leave me at once. I was on the point of crying, and only very shame seemed to keep it down. To save myself from shedding tears, I shouted terrible, wild shouts for bare life they were. I turned sick as I paused to listen; no answering sound came but the unfeeling echoes. Only the noiseless, pitiless snow kept falling thicker, thicker, faster, faster! I was growing numb and sleepy. I tried to move about, but I dared not go far, for fear of the precipices which, I knew, abounded in certain places on the Fells. Now and then, I stood still and shouted again; but my voice was getting choked with tears, as I thought of the desolate helpless death I was to die, and how little they at home, sitting round the warm, red, bright fire, wotted what was become of me, and how my poor father would grieve for me, it would surely kill him, it would break his heart, poor old man! Aunt Fanny too, was this to be the end of all her cares for me? I began to review my life in a strange kind of vivid dream, in which the various scenes of my few boyish years passed before me like visions. In a pang of agony, caused by such remembrance of my short life, I gathered up my strength and called out once more, a long, despairing, wailing cry, to which I had no hope of obtaining any answer, save from the echoes around, dulled as the sound might be by the thickened air. To my surprise I heard a cry - almost as long, as wild as mine - so wild that it seemed unearthly, and I almost thought it must be the voice of some of the mocking spirits of the Fells, about whom I had heard so many tales. My heart suddenly began to beat fast and loud. I could not reply for a minute or two. I nearly fancied I had lost the power of utterance. Just at this moment a dog barked. Was it Lassie's bark, my brother's collie? an ugly enough brute, with a white, ill-looking face, that my father always kicked whenever he saw it, partly for its own demerits, partly because it belonged to my brother. On such occasions, Gregory would whistle Lassie away, and go off and sit with her in some outhouse. My father had once or twice been ashamed of himself, when the poor collie had yowled out with the suddenness of the pain, and had relieved himself of his self-reproach by blaming my brother, who, he said, had no notion of training a dog, and was enough to ruin any collie in Christendom with his stupid way of allowing them to lie by the kitchen fire. To all which Gregory would answer nothing, nor even seem to hear, but go on looking absent and moody.

Yes! there again! It was Lassie's bark! Now or never! I lifted up my voice and shouted "Lassie! Lassie! for God's sake, Lassie!" Another moment, and the great white-faced Lassie was curving and gambolling with delight round my feet and legs, looking, however, up in my face with her intelligent, apprehensive eyes, as if fearing lest I might greet her with a blow, as I had done oftentimes before. But I cried with gladness, as I stooped down and patted her. My mind was sharing in my body's weakness, and I could not reason, but I knew that help was at hand. A gray figure came more and more distinctly out of the thick, close-pressing darkness. It was Gregory wrapped in his maud.

"Oh, Gregory!" said I, and I fell upon his neck, unable to speak another word. He never spoke much, and made me no answer for some little time. Then he told me we must move, we must walk for the dear life, we must find our road home, if possible; but we must move, or we should be frozen to death.

"Don't you know the way home?" asked I.

"I thought I did when I set out, but I am doubtful now. The snow blinds me, and I am feared that in moving about just now, I have lost the right gait homewards."

He had his shepherd's staff with him, and by dint of plunging it before us at every step we took, clinging close to each other, we went on safely enough, as far as not falling down any of the steep rocks, but it was slow, dreary work. My brother, I saw, was more guided by Lassie and the way she took than anything else, trusting to her instinct. It was too dark to see far before us; but he called her back continually, and noted from what quarter she returned, and shaped our slow steps accordingly. But the tedious motion scarcely kept my very blood from freezing. Every bone, every fibre in my body seemed first to ache, and then to swell, and then to turn numb with the intense cold. My brother bore it better than I, from having been more out upon the hills. He did not speak, except to call Lassie. I strove to be brave, and not complain; but now I felt the deadly fatal sleep stealing over me.

"I can go no farther," I said, in a drowsy tone. I remember I suddenly became dogged and resolved. Sleep I would, were it only for five minutes. If death were to be the consequence, sleep I would. Gregory stood still. I suppose, he recognized the peculiar phase of suffering to which I had been brought by the cold.

"It is of no use," said he, as if to himself. "We are no nearer home than we were when we started, as far as I can tell. Our only chance is in Lassie. Here! roll thee in my maud, lad, and lay thee down on this sheltered side of this bit of rock. Creep close under it, lad, and I'll lie by thee, and strive to keep the warmth in us. Stay! hast gotten aught about thee they'll know at home?"

I felt him unkind thus to keep me from slumber, but on his repeating the question, I pulled out my pocket-handkerchief, of some showy pattern, which Aunt Fanny had hemmed for me, Gregory took it, and tied it round Lassie's neck.

"Hie thee, Lassie, hie thee home!" And the white-faced ill-favoured brute was off like a shot in the darkness. Now I might lie down, now I might sleep. In my drowsy stupor I felt that I was being tenderly covered up by my brother; but what with I neither knew nor cared - I was too dull, too selfish, too numb to think and reason, or I might have known that in that bleak bare place there was nought to wrap me in, save what was taken off another. I was glad enough when he ceased his cares and lay down by me. I took his hand.

"Thou canst not remember, lad, how we lay together thus by our dying mother. She put thy small, wee hand in mine, I reckon she sees us now; and belike we shall soon be with her. Anyhow, God's will be done."

"Dear Gregory," I muttered, and crept nearer to him for warmth. He was talking still, and again about our mother, when I fell asleep. In an instant, or so it seemed, there were many voices about me, many faces hovering round me, the sweet luxury of warmth was stealing into every part of me. I was in my own little bed at home. I am thankful to say, my first word was "Gregory?"

A look passed from one to another my father's stern old face strove in vain to keep its sternness; his mouth quivered, his eyes filled slowly with unwonted tears.

"I would have given him half my land, I would have blessed him as my son, oh God! I would have knelt at his feet, and asked him to forgive my hardness of heart."

I heard no more. A whirl came through my brain, catching me back to death.

I came slowly to my consciousness, weeks afterwards. My father's hair was white when I recovered, and his hands shook as he looked into my face.

We spoke no more of Gregory. We could not speak of him; but he was strangely in our thoughts. Lassie came and went with never a word of blame; nay, my father would try to stroke her, but she shrank away; and he, as if reproved by the poor dumb beast, would sigh, and be silent and abstracted for a time.

Aunt Fanny, always a talker, told me all. How, on that fatal night, my father, irritated by my prolonged absence, and probably more anxious than he cared to show, had been fierce and imperious, even beyond his wont, to Gregory; had upbraided him with his father's poverty, his own stupidity which made his services good for nothing for so, in spite of the old shepherd, my father always chose to consider them. At last, Gregory had risen up, and whistled Lassie out with him--poor Lassie, crouching underneath his chair for fear of a kick or a blow. Some time before, there had been some talk between my father and my aunt respecting my return; and when aunt Fanny told me all this, she said she fancied that Gregory might have noticed the coming storm, and gone out silently to meet me. Three hours afterwards, when all were running about in wild alarm, not knowing whither to go in search of me, not even missing Gregory, or heeding his absence, poor fellow poor, poor fellow! Lassie came home, with my handkerchief tied round her neck. They knew and understood, and the whole strength of the farm was turned out to follow her, with wraps, and blankets, and brandy, and every thing that could be thought of. I lay in chilly sleep, but still alive, beneath the rock that Lassie guided them to. I was covered over with my brother's plaid, and his thick shepherd's coat was carefully wrapped round my feet. He was in his shirt-sleeves, his arm thrown over me, a quiet smile (he had hardly ever smiled in life) upon his still, cold face.

My father's last words were, "God forgive me my hardness of heart towards the fatherless child!"

And what marked the depth of his feeling of repentance, perhaps more than all, considering the passionate love he bore my mother, was this: we found a paper of directions after his death, in which he desired that he might lie at the foot of the grave, in which, by his desire, poor Gregory had been laid with OUR MOTHER.

Christmas Storms And Sunshine

In the town of ---- (no matter where) there circulated two local newspapers (no matter when). Now the Flying Post was long established and respectable - alias bigoted and Tory; the Examiner was spirited and intelligent - alias new-fangled and democratic. Every week these newspapers contained articles abusing each other; as cross and peppery as articles could be, and evidently the production of irritated minds, although they seemed to have one stereotyped commencement, "Though the article appearing in last week's Post (or Examiner) is below contempt, yet we have been induced," &c., &c., and every Saturday the Radical shopkeepers shook hands together, and agreed that the Post was done for, by the slashing, clever Examiner; while the more dignified Tories began by regretting that Johnson should think that low paper, only read by a few of the vulgar, worth wasting his wit upon; however the Examiner was at its last gasp.

It was not though. It lived and flourished; at least it paid its way, as one of the heroes of my story could tell. He was chief compositor, or whatever title may be given to the head-man of the mechanical part of a newspaper. He hardly confined himself to that department. Once or twice, unknown to the editor, when the manuscript had fallen short, he had filled up the vacant space by compositions of his own; announcements of a forthcoming crop of green peas in December; a grey thrush having been seen, or a white hare, or such interesting phenomena; invented for the occasion, I must confess; but what of that? His wife always knew when to expect a little specimen of her husband's literary talent by a peculiar cough, which served as prelude; and, judging from this encouraging sign, and the high-pitched and emphatic voice in which he read them, she was inclined to think, that an "Ode to an early Rose-bud," in the corner devoted to original poetry, and a letter in the correspondence department, signed "Pro Bono Publico," were her husband's writing, and to hold up her head accordingly.

I never could find out what it was that occasioned the Hodgsons to lodge in the same house as the Jenkinses. Jenkins held the same office in the Tory paper as Hodgson did in the Examiner, and, as I said before, I leave you to give it a name. But Jenkins had a proper sense of his position, and a proper reverence for all in authority, from the king down to the editor and sub-editor. He would as soon have thought of borrowing the king's crown for a nightcap, or the king's sceptre for a walking-stick, as he would have thought of filling up any spare corner with any production of his own; and I think it would have even added to his contempt of Hodgson (if that were possible), had he known of the "productions of his brain," as the latter fondly alluded to the paragraphs he inserted, when speaking to his wife.

Jenkins had his wife too. Wives were wanting to finish the completeness of the quarrel, which existed one memorable Christmas week, some dozen years ago, between the two neighbours, the two compositors. And with wives, it was a very pretty, a very complete quarrel. To make the opposing parties still more equal, still more well-matched, if the Hodgsons had a baby ("such a baby! a poor, puny little thing"), Mrs. Jenkins had a cat ("such a cat! a great, nasty, miowling tom-cat, that was always stealing the milk put by for little Angel's supper"). And now, having matched Greek with Greek, I must proceed to the tug of war. It was the day before Christmas; such a cold east wind! such an inky sky! such a blue-black look in people's faces, as they were driven out more than usual, to complete their purchases for the next day's festival.

Before leaving home that morning, Jenkins had given some money to his wife to buy the next day's dinner.

"My dear, I wish for turkey and sausages. It may be a weakness, but I own I am partial to sausages. My deceased mother was. Such tastes are hereditary. As to the sweets, whether plum-pudding or mince-pies, I leave such considerations to you; I only beg you not to mind expense. Christmas comes but once a year."

And again he had called out from the bottom of the first flight of stairs, just close to the Hodgsons' door ("such ostentatiousness," as Mrs. Hodgson observed), "You will not forget the sausages, my dear?"

"I should have liked to have had something above common, Mary," said Hodgson, as they too made their plans for the next day, "but I think roast beef must do for us. You see, love, we've a family."

"Only one, Jem! I don't want more than roast beef, though, I'm sure. Before I went to service, mother and me would have thought roast beef a very fine dinner."

"Well, let's settle it then, roast beef and a plum-pudding; and now, good-by. Mind and take care of little Tom. I thought he was a bit hoarse this morning."

And off he went to his work.

Now, it was a good while since Mrs. Jenkins and Mrs. Hodgson had spoken to each other, although they were quite as much in possession of the knowledge of events and opinions as though they did. Mary knew that Mrs. Jenkins despised her for not having a real lace cap, which Mrs. Jenkins had; and for having been a servant, which Mrs. Jenkins had not; and the little occasional pinchings which the Hodgsons were obliged to resort to, to make both ends meet, would have been very patiently endured by Mary, if she had not winced under Mrs. Jenkins's knowledge of such economy. But she had her revenge. She had a child, and Mrs. Jenkins had none. To have had a child, even such a puny baby as little Tom, Mrs. Jenkins would have worn commonest caps, and cleaned grates, and drudged her fingers to the bone. The great unspoken disappointment of her life soured her temper, and turned her thoughts inward, and made her morbid and selfish.

"Hang that cat! he's been stealing again! he's gnawed the cold mutton in his nasty mouth till it's not fit to set before a Christian; and I've nothing else for Jem's dinner. But I'll give it him now I've caught him, that I will!"

So saying, Mary Hodgson caught up her husband's Sunday cane, and despite pussy's cries and scratches, she gave him such a beating as she hoped might cure him of his thievish propensities; when lo! and behold, Mrs. Jenkins stood at the door with a face of bitter wrath.

"Aren't you ashamed of yourself, ma'am, to abuse a poor dumb animal, ma'am, as knows no better than to take food when he sees it, ma'am? He only follows the nature which God has given, ma'am; and it's a pity your nature, ma'am, which I've heard, is of the stingy saving species, does not make you shut your cupboard-door a little closer. There is such a thing as law for brute animals. I'll ask Mr. Jenkins, but I don't think them Radicals has done away with that law yet, for all their Reform Bill, ma'am. My poor precious love of a Tommy, is he hurt? and is his leg broke for taking a mouthful of scraps, as most people would give away to a beggar, if he'd take 'em?" wound up Mrs. Jenkins, casting a contemptuous look on the remnant of a scrag end of mutton.

Mary felt very angry and very guilty. For she really pitied the poor limping animal as he crept up to his mistress, and there lay down to bemoan himself; she wished she had not beaten him so hard, for it certainly was her own careless way of never shutting the cupboard-door that had tempted him to his fault. But the sneer at her little bit of mutton turned her penitence to fresh wrath, and she shut the door in Mrs. Jenkins's face, as she stood caressing her cat in the lobby, with such a bang, that it wakened little Tom, and he began to cry.

Everything was to go wrong with Mary to-day. Now baby was awake, who was to take her husband's dinner to the office? She took the child in her arms, and tried to hush him off to sleep again, and as she sung she cried, she could hardly tell why, a sort of reaction from her violent angry feelings. She wished she had never beaten the poor cat; she wondered if his leg was really broken. What would her mother say if she knew how cross and cruel her little Mary was getting? If she should live to beat her child in one of her angry fits?

It was of no use lullabying while she sobbed so; it must be given up, and she must just carry her baby in her arms, and take him with her to the office, for it was long past dinner-time. So she pared the mutton carefully, although by so doing she reduced the meat to an infinitesimal quantity, and taking the baked potatoes out of the oven, she popped them piping hot into her basket with the et-cæteras of plate, butter, salt, and knife and fork.

It was, indeed, a bitter wind. She bent against it as she ran, and the flakes of snow were sharp and cutting as ice. Baby cried all the way, though she cuddled him up in her shawl. Then her husband had made his appetite up for a potato pie, and (literary man as he was) his body got so much the better of his mind, that he looked rather black at the cold mutton. Mary had no appetite for her own dinner when she arrived at home again. So, after she had tried to feed baby, and he had fretfully refused to take his bread and milk, she laid him down as usual on his quilt, surrounded by playthings, while she sided away, and chopped suet for the next day's pudding. Early in the afternoon a parcel came, done up first in brown paper, then in such a white, grass-bleached, sweet-smelling towel, and a note from her dear, dear mother; in which quaint writing she endeavoured to tell her daughter that she was not forgotten at Christmas time; but that learning that Farmer Burton was killing his pig, she had made interest for some of his famous pork, out of which she had manufactured some sausages, and flavoured them just as Mary used to like when she lived at home.

"Dear, dear mother!" said Mary to herself. "There never was any one like her for remembering other folk. What rare sausages she used to make! Home things have a smack with 'em, no bought things can ever have. Set them up with their sausages! I've a notion if Mrs. Jenkins had ever tasted mother's she'd have no fancy for them town-made things Fanny took in just now."

And so she went on thinking about home, till the smiles and the dimples came out again at the remembrance of that pretty cottage, which would look green even now in the depth of winter, with its pyracanthus, and its holly-bushes, and the great Portugal laurel that was her mother's pride. And the back path through the orchard to Farmer Burton's; how well she remembered it. The bushels of unripe apples she had picked up there, and distributed among his pigs, till he had scolded her for giving them so much green trash.

She was interrupted, her baby (I call him a baby, because his father and mother did, and because he was so little of his age, but I rather think he was eighteen months old,) had fallen asleep some time before among his playthings; an uneasy, restless sleep; but of which Mary had been thankful, as his morning's nap had been too short, and as she was so busy. But now he began to make such a strange crowing noise, just like a chair drawn heavily and gratingly along a kitchen-floor! His eyes was open, but expressive of nothing but pain.

"Mother's darling!" said Mary, in terror, lifting him up. "Baby, try not to make that noise. Hush, hush, darling; what hurts him?" But the noise came worse and worse.

"Fanny! Fanny!" Mary called in mortal fright, for her baby was almost black with his gasping breath, and she had no one to ask for aid or sympathy but her landlady's daughter, a little girl of twelve or thirteen, who attended to the house in her mother's absence, as daily cook in gentlemen's families. Fanny was more especially considered the attendant of the upstairs lodgers (who paid for the use of the kitchin, "for Jenkins could not abide the smell of meat cooking"), but just now she was fortunately sitting at her afternoon's work of darning stockings, and hearing Mrs. Hodgson's cry of terror, she ran to her sitting-room, and understood the case at a glance.

"He's got the croup! Oh, Mrs. Hodgson, he'll die as sure as fate. Little brother had it, and he died in no time. The doctor said he could do nothing for him, it had gone too far. He said if we'd put him in a warm bath at first, it might have saved him; but, bless you! he was never half so bad as your baby."

Unconsciously there mingled in her statement some of a child's love of producing an effect; but the increasing danger was clear enough.

"Oh, my baby! my baby! Oh, love, love! don't look so ill; I cannot bear it. And my fire so low! There, I was thinking of home, and picking currants, and never minding the fire. Oh, Fanny! what is the fire like in the kitchen? Speak."

"Mother told me to screw it up, and throw some slack on as soon as Mrs. Jenkins had done with it, and so I did. It's very low and black. But, oh, Mrs. Hodgson! let me run for the doctor, I cannot abear to hear him, it's so like little brother."

Through her streaming tears Mary motioned her to go; and trembling, sinking, sick at heart, she laid her boy in his cradle, and ran to fill her kettle.

Mrs. Jenkins, having cooked her husband's snug little dinner, to which he came home; having told him her story of pussy's beating, at which he was justly and dignifiedly indignant, saying it was all of a piece with that abusive Examiner; having received the sausages, and turkey, and mince pies, which her husband had ordered; and cleaned up the room, and prepared everything for tea, and coaxed and duly bemoaned her cat (who had pretty nearly forgotten his beating, but very much enjoyed the petting), having done all these and many other things, Mrs. Jenkins sate down to get up the real lace cap. Every thread was pulled out separately, and carefully stretched: when, what was that? Outside, in the street, a chorus of piping children's voices sang the old carol she had heard a hundred times in the days of her youth:--

"As Joseph was a walking he heard an angel sing,
'This night shall be born our heavenly King.
He neither shall be born in housen nor in hall,
Nor in the place of Paradise, but in an ox's stall.
He neither shall be clothed in purple nor in pall,
But all in fair linen, as were babies all:
He neither shall be rocked in silver nor in gold,
But in a wooden cradle that rocks on the mould,'" &c.

She got up and went to the window. There, below, stood the group of grey black little figures, relieved against the snow, which now enveloped everything. "For old sake's sake," as she phrased it, she counted out a halfpenny apiece for the singers, out of the copper bag, and threw them down below.

The room had become chilly while she had been counting out and throwing down her money, so she stirred her already glowing fire, and sat down right before it but not to stretch her lace; like Mary Hodgson, she began to think over long-past days, on softening remembrances of the dead and gone, on words long forgotten, on holy stories heard at her mother's knee.

"I cannot think what's come over me to-night," said she, half aloud, recovering herself by the sound of her own voice from her train of thought "My head goes wandering on them old times. I'm sure more texts have come into my head with thinking on my mother within this last half hour, than I've thought on for years and years. I hope I'm not going to die. Folks say, thinking too much on the dead betokens we're going to join 'em; I should be loth to go just yet, such a fine turkey as we've got for dinner to-morrow, too!"

Knock, knock, knock, at the door, as fast as knuckles could go. And then, as if the comer could not wait, the door was opened, and Mary Hodgson stood there as white as death.

"Mrs. Jenkins! oh, your kettle is boiling, thank God! Let me have the water for my baby, for the love of God! He's got croup, and is dying!"

Mrs. Jenkins turned on her chair with a wooden inflexible look on her face, that (between ourselves) her husband knew and dreaded for all his pompous dignity.

"I'm sorry I can't oblige you, ma'am; my kettle is wanted for my husband's tea. Don't be afeared, Tommy, Mrs. Hodgson won't venture to intrude herself where she's not desired. You'd better send for the doctor, ma'am, instead of wasting your time in wringing your hands, ma'am - my kettle is engaged."

Mary clasped her hands together with passionate force, but spoke no word of entreaty to that wooden face--that sharp, determined voice; but, as she turned away, she prayed for strength to bear the coming trial, and strength to forgive Mrs. Jenkins.

Mrs. Jenkins watched her go away meekly, as one who has no hope, and then she turned upon herself as sharply as she ever did on any one else.

"What a brute I am, Lord forgive me! What's my husband's tea to a baby's life? In croup, too, where time is everything. You crabbed old vixen, you! any one may know you never had a child!"

She was down stairs (kettle in hand) before she had finished her self-upbraiding; and when in Mrs. Hodgson's room, she rejected all thanks (Mary had not the voice for many words), saying, stiffly, "I do it for the poor babby's sake, ma'am, hoping he may live to have mercy to poor dumb beasts, if he does forget to lock his cupboards."

But she did everything, and more than Mary, with her young inexperience, could have thought of. She prepared the warm bath, and tried it with her husband's own thermometer (Mr. Jenkins was as punctual as clockwork in noting down the temperature of every day). She let his mother place her baby in the tub, still preserving the same rigid, affronted aspect, and then she went upstairs without a word. Mary longed to ask her to stay, but dared not; though, when she left the room, the tears chased each other down her cheeks faster than ever. Poor young mother! how she counted the minutes till the doctor should come. But, before he came, down again stalked Mrs. Jenkins, with something in her hand.

"I've seen many of these croup-fits, which, I take it, you've not, ma'am. Mustard plaisters is very sovereign, put on the throat; I've been up and made one, ma'am, and, by your leave, I'll put it on the poor little fellow."

Mary could not speak, but she signed her grateful assent.

It began to smart while they still kept silence; and he looked up to his mother as if seeking courage from her looks to bear the stinging pain; but she was softly crying, to see him suffer, and her want of courage reacted upon him, and he began to sob aloud. Instantly Mrs. Jenkins's apron was up, hiding her face: "Peep-bo, baby," said she, as merrily as she could. His little face brightened, and his mother having once got the cue, the two women kept the little fellow amused, until his plaister had taken effect.

"He's better, oh, Mrs. Jenkins, look at his eyes! how different! And he breathes quite softly -"

As Mary spoke thus, the doctor entered. He examined his patient. Baby was really better.

"It has been a sharp attack, but the remedies you have applied have been worth all the Pharmacopoeia an hour later. I shall send a powder."

Mrs. Jenkins stayed to hear this opinion; and (her heart wonderfully more easy) was going to leave the room, when Mary seized her hand and kissed it; she could not speak her gratitude.

Mrs. Jenkins looked affronted and awkward, and as if she must go upstairs and wash her hand directly.

But, in spite of these sour looks, she came softly down an hour or so afterwards to see how baby was.

The little gentleman slept well after the fright he had given his friends; and on Christmas morning, when Mary awoke and looked at the sweet little pale face lying on her arm, she could hardly realize the danger he had been in.

When she came down (later than usual), she found the household in a commotion. What do you think had happened? Why, pussy had been a traitor to his best friend, and eaten up some of Mr. Jenkins's own especial sausages; and gnawed and tumbled the rest so, that they were not fit to be eaten! There were no bounds to that cat's appetite! he would have eaten his own father if he had been tender enough. And now Mrs. Jenkins stormed and cried "Hang the cat!"

Christmas Day, too! and all the shops shut! "What was turkey without sausages?" gruffly asked Mr. Jenkins.

"Oh, Jem!" whispered Mary, "hearken what a piece of work he's making about sausages, I should like to take Mrs. Jenkins up some of mother's; they're twice as good as bought sausages."

"I see no objection, my dear. Sausages do not involve intimacies, else his politics are what I can no ways respect."

"But, oh, Jem, if you had seen her last night about baby! I'm sure she may scold me for ever, and I'll not answer. I'd even make her cat welcome to the sausages." The tears gathered to Mary's eyes as she kissed her boy.

"Better take 'em upstairs, my dear, and give them to the cat's mistress." And Jem chuckled at his saying.

Mary put them on a plate, but still she loitered.

"What must I say, Jem? I never know."

"Say - I hope you'll accept of these sausages, as my mother no, that's not grammar; say what comes uppermost, Mary, it will be sure to be right."

So Mary carried them upstairs and knocked at the door; and when told to "come in," she looked very red, but went up to Mrs. Jenkins, saying, "Please take these. Mother made them." And was away before an answer could be given.

Just as Hodgson was ready to go to church, Mrs. Jenkins came downstairs, and called Fanny. In a minute, the latter entered the Hodgsons' room, and delivered Mr. and Mrs. Jenkins's compliments, and they would be particular glad if Mr. and Mrs. Hodgson would eat their dinner with them.

"And carry baby upstairs in a shawl, be sure," added Mrs. Jenkins's voice in the passage, close to the door, whither she had followed her messenger. There was no discussing the matter, with the certainty of every word being overheard.

Mary looked anxiously at her husband. She remembered his saying he did not approve of Mr. Jenkins's politics.

"Do you think it would do for baby?" asked he.

"Oh, yes," answered she, eagerly; "I would wrap him up so warm."

"And I've got our room up to sixty-five already, for all it's so frosty," added the voice outside.

Now, how do you think they settled the matter? The very best way in the world. Mr. and Mrs. Jenkins came down into the Hodgsons' room, and dined there. Turkey at the top, roast beef at the bottom, sausages at one side, potatoes at the other. Second course, plum-pudding at the top, and mince pies at the bottom.

And after dinner, Mrs. Jenkins would have baby on her knee; and he seemed quite to take to her; she declared he was admiring the real lace on her cap, but Mary thought (though she did not say so) that he was pleased by her kind looks and coaxing words. Then he was wrapped up and carried carefully upstairs to tea, in Mrs. Jenkins's room. And after tea, Mrs. Jenkins, and Mary, and her husband, found out each other's mutual liking for music, and sat singing old glees and catches, till I don't know what o'clock, without one word of politics or newspapers.

Before they parted, Mary had coaxed pussy on to her knee; for Mrs. Jenkins would not part with baby, who was sleeping on her lap.

"When you're busy, bring him to me. Do, now, it will be a real favour. I know you must have a deal to do, with another coming; let him come up to me. I'll take the greatest of cares of him; pretty darling, how sweet he looks when he's asleep!"

When the couples were once more alone, the husbands unburdened their minds to their wives.

Mr. Jenkins said to his--"Do you know, Burgess tried to make me believe Hodgson was such a fool as to put paragraphs into the Examiner now and then; but I see he knows his place, and has got too much sense to do any such thing."

Hodgson said "Mary, love, I almost fancy from Jenkins's way of speaking (so much civiler than I expected), he guesses I wrote that 'Pro Bono' and the 'Rose-bud,' at any rate, I've no objection to your naming it, if the subject should come uppermost; I should like him to know I'm a literary man."

Well! I've ended my tale; I hope you don't think it too long; but, before I go, just let me say one thing.

If any of you have any quarrels, or misunderstandings, or coolnesses, or cold shoulders, or shynesses, or tiffs, or miffs, or huffs, with any one else, just make friends before Christmas, you will be so much merrier if you do.

I ask it of you for the sake of that old angelic song, heard so many years ago by the shepherds, keeping watch by night, on Bethlehem Heights.

Hand On Heart

"Mother, I should so like to have a great deal of money," said little Tom Fletcher one evening, as he sat on a low stool by his mother's knee. His mother was knitting busily by the firelight, and they had both been silent for some time.

"What would you do with a great deal of money if you had it?"

"Oh! I don't know, I would do a great many things. But should not you like to have a great deal of money, mother?" persisted he.

"Perhaps I should," answered Mrs. Fletcher. "I am like you sometimes, dear, and think that I should be very glad of a little more money. But then I don't think I am like you in one thing, for I have always some little plan in my mind, for which I should want the money. I never wish for it just for its own sake."

"Why, mother! there are so many things we could do if we had but money; real good, wise things I mean."

"And if we have real good, wise things in our head to do, which cannot be done without money, I can quite enter into the wish for money. But you know, my little boy, you did not tell me of any good or wise thing."

"No! I believe I was not thinking of good or wise things just then, but only how much I should like money to do what I liked," answered little Tom ingenuously, looking up in his mother's face. She smiled down upon him, and stroked his head. He knew she was pleased with him for having told her openly what was passing in his mind. Presently he began again.

"Mother, if you wanted to do something very good and wise, and if you could not do it without money, what should you do?"

"There are two ways of obtaining money for such wants; one is by earning; and the other is by saving. Now both are good, because both imply self-denial. Do you understand me, Tom? If you have to earn money, you must steadily go on doing what you do not like perhaps; such as working when you would like to be playing, or in bed, or sitting talking with me over the fire. You deny yourself these little pleasures; and that is a good habit in itself, to say nothing of the industry and energy you have to exert in working. If you save money, you can easily see how you exercise self-denial. You do without something you wish for in order to possess the money it would have cost. Inasmuch as self-denial, energy, and industry are all good things, you do well either to earn or to save. But you see the purpose for which you want the money must be taken into consideration. You say, for 'something wise and good.' Either earning or saving becomes holy in this case. I must then think which will be most consistent with my other duties, before I decide whether I will earn or save money."

"I don't quite know what you mean, mother."

"I will try and explain myself. You know I have to keep a little shop, and to try and get employment in knitting stockings, and to clean my house, and to mend our clothes, and many other things. Now, do you think I should be doing my duty if I left you in the evenings, when you come home from school, to go out as a waiter at ladies' parties? I could earn a good deal of money by it, and I could spend it well among those who are poorer than I am (such as lame Harry), but then I should be leaving you alone in the little time that we have to be together; I do not think I should be doing right even for our 'good and wise purpose' to earn money, if it took me away from you at nights: do you, Tom?"

"No, indeed; you never mean to do it, do you, mother?"

"No," said she, smiling; "at any rate not till you are older. You see at present then, I cannot earn money, if I want a little more than usual to help a sick neighbour. I must then try and save money. Nearly every one can do that."

"Can we, mother? We are so careful of everything. Ned Dixon calls us stingy: what could we save?"

"Oh, many and many a little thing. We use many things which are luxuries; which we do not want, but only use them for pleasure. Tea and sugar, butter, our Sunday's dinner of bacon or meat, the grey ribbon I bought for my bonnet, because you thought it prettier than the black, which was cheaper; all these are luxuries. We use very little tea or sugar, it is true; but we might do without any."

"You did do without any, mother, for a long, long time, you know, to help widow Black; it was only for your bad head-aches."

"Well! but you see we can save money; a penny, a halfpenny a day, or even a penny a week, would in time make a little store ready to be applied to the 'good and wise' purpose, when the time comes. But do you know, my little boy, I think we may be considering money too much as the only thing required if we want to do a kindness."

"If it is not the only thing, it is the chief thing, at any rate."

"No, love, it is not the chief thing. I should think very poorly of that beggar who liked sixpence given with a curse (as I have sometimes heard it), better than the kind and gentle words some people use in refusing to give. The curse sinks deep into the heart; or if it does not, it is a proof that the poor creature has been made hard before by harsh treatment. And mere money can do little to cheer a sore heart. It is kindness only that can do this. Now we have all of us kindness in our power. The little child of two years old, who can only just totter about, can show kindness?"

"Can I, mother?"

"To be sure, dear; and you often do, only perhaps not quite so often as you might do. Neither do I. But instead of wishing for money (of which I don't think either you or I are ever likely to have much), suppose you try to-morrow how you can make people happier, by thinking of little loving actions of help. Let us try and take for our text, 'Silver and gold I have none, but such as I have give I unto thee.'"

"Ay, mother, we will."

Must I tell you about little Tom's "to-morrow."

I do not know if little Tom dreamed of what his mother and he had been talking about, but I do know that the first thing he thought about, when he awoke in the morning, was his mother's saying that he might try how many kind actions he could do that day without money; and he was so impatient to begin, that he jumped up and dressed himself, although it was more than an hour before his usual time of getting up. All the time he kept wondering what a little boy like him, only eight years old, could do for other people; till at last he grew so puzzled with inventing occasions for showing kindness, that he very wisely determined to think no more about it, but learn his lessons very perfectly; that was the first thing he had to do; and then he would try, without too much planning beforehand, to keep himself ready to lend a helping hand, or to give a kind word, when the right time came. So he screwed himself into a corner, out of the way of his mother's sweeping and dusting, and tucked his feet up on the rail of the chair, turned his face to the wall, and in about half an hour's time, he could turn round with a light heart, feeling he had learnt his lesson well, and might employ his time as he liked till breakfast was ready. He looked round the room; his mother had arranged all neatly, and was now gone to the bedroom; but the coal-scuttle and the can for water were empty, and Tom ran away to fill them; and as he came back with the latter from the pump, he saw Ann Jones (the scold of the neighbourhood) hanging out her clothes on a line stretched across from side to side of the little court, and speaking very angrily and loudly to her little girl, who was getting into some mischief in the house-place, as her mother perceived through the open door.

"There never were such plagues as my children are, to be sure," said Ann Jones, as she went into her house, looking very red and passionate.
Directly after, Tom heard the sound of a slap, and then a little child's cry of pain.

"I wonder," thought he, "if I durst go and offer to nurse and play with little Hester. Ann Jones is fearful cross, and just as likely to take me wrong as right; but she won't box me for mother's sake; mother nursed Jemmy many a day through the fever, so she won't slap me, I think. Any rate, I'll try." But it was with a beating heart he said to the fierce-looking Mrs. Jones, "Please, may I go and play with Hester. May be I could keep her quiet while you're busy hanging out clothes."

"What! and let you go slopping about, I suppose, just when I'd made all ready for my master's breakfast. Thank you, but my own children's mischief is as much as I reckon on; I'll have none of strange lads in my house."

"I did not mean to do mischief or slop," said Tom, a little sadly at being misunderstood in his good intentions. "I only wanted to help."

"If you want to help, lift me up those clothes' pegs, and save me stooping; my back's broken with it."

Tom would much rather have gone to play with and amuse little Hester; but it was true enough that giving Mrs. Jones the clothes' pegs as she wanted them would help her as much; and perhaps keep her from being so cross with her children if they did anything to hinder her. Besides, little Hester's cry had died away, and she was evidently occupied in some new pursuit (Tom could only hope that it was not in mischief this time); so he began to give Ann the pegs as she wanted them, and she, soothed by his kind help, opened her heart a little to him.

"I wonder how it is your mother has trained you up to be so handy, Tom; you're as good as a girl, better than many a girl. I don't think Hester in three years' time will be as thoughtful as you. There!" (as a fresh scream reached them from the little ones inside the house), "they are at some mischief again; but I'll teach 'em," said she, getting down from her stool in a fresh access of passion.

"Let me go," said Tom, in a begging voice, for he dreaded the cruel sound of another slap. "I'll lift the basket of pegs on to a stool, so that you need not stoop; and I'll keep the little ones safe out of mischief till you're done. Do let me go, missus."

With some grumblings at losing his help, she let him go into the house-place. He found Hester, a little girl of five, and two younger ones.

They had been fighting for a knife, and in the struggle, the second, Johnnie, had cut his finger - not very badly, but he was frightened at the sight of the blood; and Hester, who might have helped, and who was really sorry, stood sullenly aloof, dreading the scolding her mother always gave her if either of the little ones hurt themselves while under her care.

"Hester," said Tom, "will you get me some cold water, please? it will stop the bleeding better than anything. I daresay you can find me a basin to hold it."

Hester trotted off, pleased at Tom's confidence in her power. When the bleeding was partly stopped, he asked her to find him a bit of rag, and she scrambled under the dresser for a little piece she had hidden there the day before.

Meanwhile, Johnny ceased crying, he was so interested in all the preparation for dressing his little wound, and so much pleased to find himself an object of so much attention and consequence. The baby, too, sat on the floor, gravely wondering at the commotion; and thus busily occupied, they were quiet and out of mischief till Ann Jones came in, and, having hung out her clothes, and finished that morning's piece of work, she was ready to attend to her children in her rough, hasty kind of way.

"Well! I'm sure, Tom, you've tied it up as neatly as I could have done. I wish I'd always such an one as you to see after the children; but you must run off now, lad, your mother was calling you as I came in, and I said I'd send you; good-by, and thank you."

As Tom was going away, the baby, sitting in square gravity on the floor, but somehow conscious of Tom's gentle helpful ways, put up her mouth to be kissed; and he stooped down in answer to the little gesture, feeling very happy, and very full of love and kindliness.

After breakfast, his mother told him it was school time, and he must set off, as she did not like him to run in out of breath and flurried, just when the schoolmaster was going to begin; but she wished him to come in decently and in order, with quiet decorum, and thoughtfulness as to what he was going to do. So Tom got his cap and his bag, and went off with a light heart, which I suppose made his footsteps light, for he found himself above half way to school while it wanted yet a quarter to the time. So he slackened his pace, and looked about him a little more than he had been doing. There was a little girl on the other side of the street carrying a great big basket, and lugging along a little child just able to walk; but who, I suppose, was tired, for he was crying pitifully, and sitting down every two or three steps. Tom ran across the street, for, as perhaps you have found out, he was very fond of babies, and could not bear to hear them cry.

"Little girl, what is he crying about? Does he want to be carried? I'll take him up, and carry him as far as I go alongside of you."

So saying, Tom was going to suit the action to the word; but the baby did not choose that any one should carry him but his sister, and refused Tom's kindness. Still he could carry the heavy basket of potatoes for the little girl, which he did as far as their road lay together, when she thanked him, and bade him good-by, and said she could manage very well now, her home was so near. So Tom went into school very happy and peaceful; and had a good character to take home to his mother for that morning's lesson.

It happened that this very day was the weekly half-holiday, so that Tom had many hours unoccupied that afternoon. Of course, his first employment after dinner was to learn his lessons for the next day; and then, when he had put his books away, he began to wonder what he should do next.

He stood lounging against the door wishing all manner of idle wishes; a habit he was apt to fall into. He wished he were the little boy who lived opposite, who had three brothers ready to play with him on half-holidays; he wished he were Sam Harrison, whose father had taken him one day a trip by the railroad; he wished he were the little boy who always went with the omnibuses, it must be so pleasant to go riding about on the step, and to see so many people; he wished he were a sailor, to sail away to the countries where grapes grew wild, and monkeys and parrots were to be had for the catching. Just as he was wishing himself the little Prince of Wales, to drive about in a goat-carriage, and wondering if he should not feel very shy with the three great ostrich-feathers always niddle-noddling on his head, for people to know him by, his mother came from washing up the dishes, and saw him deep in the reveries little boys and girls are apt to fall into when they are the only children in a house.

"My dear Tom," said she, "why don't you go out, and make the most of this fine afternoon?"

"Oh, mother," answered he (suddenly recalled to the fact that he was little Tom Fletcher, instead of the Prince of Wales, and consequently feeling a little bit flat), "it is so dull going out by myself. I have no one to play with. Can't you go with me, mother just this once, into the fields?"

Poor Mrs. Fletcher heartily wished she could gratify this very natural desire of her little boy; but she had the shop to mind, and many a little thing besides to do; it was impossible. But however much she might regret a thing, she was too faithful to repine. So, after a moment's thought, she said, cheerfully, "Go into the fields for a walk, and see how many wild flowers you can bring me home, and I'll get down father's jug for you to put them in when you come back."

"But, mother, there are so few pretty flowers near a town," said Tom, a little unwillingly, for it was a coming down from being Prince of Wales, and he was not yet quite reconciled to it.

"Oh dear! there are a great many if you'll only look for them. I dare say you'll make me up as many as twenty different kinds."

"Will you reckon daisies, mother?"

"To be sure; they are just as pretty as any."

"Oh, if you'll reckon such as them, I dare say I can bring you more than twenty."

So off he ran; his mother watching him till he was out of sight, and then she returned to her work. In about two hours he came back, his pale cheeks looking quite rosy, and his eyes quite bright. His country walk, taken with cheerful spirits, had done him all the good his mother desired, and had restored his usually even, happy temper.

"Look, mother! here are three-and-twenty different kinds; you said I might count all, so I have even counted this thing like a nettle with lilac flowers, and this little common blue thing."

"Robin-run-in-the-hedge is its name," said his mother. "It's very pretty if you look at it close. One, two, three" she counted them all over, and there really were three-and-twenty. She went to reach down the best jug.

"Mother," said little Tom, "do you like them very much?"

"Yes, very much," said she, not understanding his meaning. He was silent, and gave a little sigh. "Why, my dear?"

"Oh, only--it does not signify if you like them very much; but I thought how nice it would be to take them to lame Harry, who can never walk so far as the fields, and can hardly know what summer is like, I think."

"Oh, that will be very nice; I am glad you thought of it."

Lame Harry was sitting by himself, very patiently, in a neighbouring cellar. He was supported by his daughter's earnings; but as she worked in a factory, he was much alone.

If the bunch of flowers had looked pretty in the fields, they looked ten times as pretty in the cellar to which they were now carried. Lame Harry's eyes brightened up with pleasure at the sight; and he began to talk of the times long ago, when he was a little boy in the country, and had a corner of his father's garden to call his own, and grow lad's-love and wall-flower in. Little Tom put them in water for him, and put the jug on the table by him; on which his daughter had placed the old Bible, worn with much reading, although treated with careful reverence. It was lying open, with Harry's horn spectacles put in to mark the place.

"I reckon my spectacles are getting worn out; they are not so clear as they used to be; they are dim-like before my eyes, and it hurts me to read long together," said Harry. "It's a sad miss to me. I never thought the time long when I could read; but now I keep wearying for the day to be over, though the nights, when I cannot sleep for my legs paining me, are almost as bad. However, it's the Lord's will."

"Would you like me, I cannot read very well aloud, but I'd do my best, if you'd like me to read a bit to you. I'll just run home and get my tea, and be back directly." And off Tom ran.

He found it very pleasant reading aloud to lame Harry, for the old man had so much to say that was worth listening to, and was so glad of a listener, that I think there was as much talking as reading done that evening. But the Bible served as a text-book to their conversation; for in a long life old Harry had seen and heard so much, which he had connected with events, or promises, or precepts contained in the Scriptures, that it was quite curious to find how everything was brought in and dove-tailed, as an illustration of what they were reading.

When Tom got up to go away, lame Harry gave him many thanks, and told him he would not sleep the worse for having made an old man's evening so pleasant. Tom came home in high self-satisfaction. "Mother," said he, "it's all very true what you said about the good that may be done without money: I've done many pieces of good to-day without a farthing. First," said he, taking hold of his little finger, "I helped Ann Jones with hanging out her clothes when she was"

His mother had been listening while she turned over the pages of the New Testament which lay by her, and now having found what she wanted, she put her arm gently round his waist, and drew him fondly towards her. He saw her finger put under one passage, and read,

"Let not thy left hand know what thy right hand doeth."

He was silent in a moment.

Then his mother spoke in her soft low voice: "Dearest Tom, though I don't want us to talk about it, as if you had been doing more than just what you ought, I am glad you have seen the truth of what I said; how far more may be done by the loving heart than by mere money-giving; and every one may have the loving heart."

I have told you of one day of little Tom's life, when he was eight years old, and lived with his mother. I must now pass over a year, and tell you of a very different kind of life he had then to lead. His mother had never been very strong, and had had a good deal of anxiety; at last she was taken ill, and soon felt that there was no hope for her recovery.

For a long time the thought of leaving her little boy was a great distress to her, and a great trial to her faith. But God strengthened her, and sent his peace into her soul, and before her death she was content to leave her precious child in his hands, who is a Father to the fatherless, and defendeth the cause of the widow.

When she felt that she had not many more days to live, she sent for her husband's brother, who lived in a town not many miles off; and gave her little Tom in charge to him to bring up.

"There are a few pounds in the savings-bank, I don't know how many exactly and the furniture and bit of stock in the shop; perhaps they would be enough to bring him up to be a joiner, like his father before him."

She spoke feebly, and with many pauses. Her brother-in-law, though a rough kind of man, wished to do all he could to make her feel easy in her last moments, and touched with the reference to his dead brother, promised all she required.

"I'll take him back with me after" the funeral, he was going to say, but he stopped. She smiled gently, fully understanding his meaning.

"We shall, may be, not be so tender with him as you've been; but I'll see he comes to no harm. It will be a good thing for him to rough it a bit with other children, he's too nesh for a boy; but I'll pay them if they aren't kind to him in the long run, never fear."

Though this speech was not exactly what she liked, there was quite enough of good feeling in it to make her thankful for such a protector and friend for her boy. And so, thankful for the joys she had had, and thankful for the sorrows which had taught her meekness, thankful for life, and thankful for death, she died.

Her brother-in-law arranged all as she had wished. After the quiet simple funeral was over, he took Tom by the hand, and set off on the six-mile walk to his home. Tom had cried till he could cry no more, but sobs came quivering up from his heart every now and then, as he passed some well-remembered cottage, or thorn-bush, or tree on the road. His uncle was very sorry for him, but did not know what to say, or how to comfort him.

"Now mind, lad, thou com'st to me if thy cousins are o'er hard upon thee. Let me hear if they misuse thee, and I'll give it them."

Tom shrunk from the idea that this gave him of the cousins, whose companionship he had, until then, been looking forward to as a pleasure. He was not reassured when, after threading several streets and by-ways, they came into a court of dingy-looking houses, and his uncle opened the door of one, from which the noise of loud, if not angry voices was heard.

A tall large woman was whirling one child out of her way with a rough movement of her arm; while she was scolding a boy a little older than Tom, who stood listening sullenly to her angry words.

"I'll tell father of thee, I will," said she; and turning to uncle John, she began to pour out her complaints against Jack, without taking any notice of little Tom, who clung to his uncle's hand as to a protector in the scene of violence into which he had entered.

"Well, well, wife! I'll leather Jack the next time I catch him letting the water out of the pipe; but now get this lad and me some tea, for
we're weary and tired."

His aunt seemed to wish Jack might be leathered now, and to be angry with her husband for not revenging her injuries; for an injury it was that the boy had done her in letting the water all run off, and that on the very eve of the washing day. The mother grumbled as she left off mopping the wet floor, and went to the fire to stir it up ready for the kettle, without a word of greeting to her little nephew, or of welcome to her husband. On the contrary, she complained of the trouble of getting tea ready afresh, just when she had put slack on the fire, and had no water in the house to fill the kettle with. Her husband grew angry, and Tom was frightened to hear his uncle speaking sharply.

"If I can't have a cup of tea in my own house without all this ado, I'll go to the Spread Eagle, and take Tom with me. They've a bright fire there at all times, choose how they manage it; and no scolding wives. Come, Tom, let's be off."

Jack had been trying to scrape acquaintance with his cousin by winks and grimaces behind his mother's back, and now made a sign of drinking out of an imaginary glass. But Tom clung to his uncle, and softly pulled him down again on his chair, from which he had risen to go to the public-house.

"If you please, ma'am," said he, sadly frightened of his aunt, "I think I could find the pump, if you'd let me try."

She muttered something like an acquiescence; so Tom took up the kettle, and, tired as he was, went out to the pump. Jack, who had done nothing but mischief all day, stood amazed, but at last settled that his cousin was a "softy."

When Tom came back, he tried to blow the fire with the broken bellows, and at last the water boiled, and the tea was made. "Thou'rt a rare lad, Tom," said his uncle. "I wonder when our Jack will be of as much use."

This comparison did not please either Jack or his mother, who liked to keep to herself the privilege of directing their father's dissatisfaction with his children. Tom felt their want of kindliness towards him; and now that he had nothing to do but rest and eat, he began to feel very sad, and his eyes kept filling with tears, which he brushed away with the back of his hand, not wishing to have them seen. But his uncle noticed him.

"Thou had'st better have had a glass at the Spread Eagle," said he, compassionately.

"No; I only am rather tired. May I go to bed?" said he, longing for a good cry unobserved under the bed-clothes.

"Where's he to sleep?" asked the husband of the wife.

"Nay," said she, still offended on Jack's account, "that's thy look-out. He's thy flesh and blood, not mine."

"Come, wife," said uncle John, "he's an orphan, poor chap. An orphan is kin to every one."

She was softened directly, for she had much kindness in her, although this evening she had been so much put out.

"There's no place for him but with Jack and Dick. We've the baby, and the other three are packed close enough."

She took Tom up to the little back room, and stopped to talk with him for a minute or two, for her husband's words had smitten her heart, and she was sorry for the ungracious reception she had given Tom at first.

"Jack and Dick are never in bed till we come, and it's work enough to catch them then on fine evenings," said she, as she took the candle away.

Tom tried to speak to God as his mother had taught him, out of the fulness of his little heart, which was heavy enough that night. He tried to think how she would have wished him to speak and to do, and when he felt puzzled with the remembrance of the scene of disorder and anger which he had seen, he earnestly prayed God would make and keep clear his path before him. And then he fell asleep.

He had had a long dream of other and happier days, and had thought he was once more taking a Sunday evening walk with his mother, when he was roughly wakened up by his cousins.

"I say, lad, you're lying right across the bed. You must get up, and let Dick and me come in, and then creep into the space that's left."

Tom got up dizzy and half awake. His cousins got into bed, and then squabbled about the largest share. It ended in a kicking match, during which Tom stood shivering by the bedside.

"I'm sure we're pinched enough as it is," said Dick at last. "And why they've put Tom in with us I can't think. But I'll not stand it. Tom shan't sleep with us. He may lie on the floor, if he likes. I'll not hinder him."

He expected an opposition from Tom, and was rather surprised when he heard the little fellow quietly lie down, and cover himself as well as he could with his clothes. After some more quarrelling, Jack and Dick fell asleep. But in the middle of the night Dick awoke, and heard by Tom's breathing that he was still awake, and was crying gently.

"What! molly-coddle, crying for a softer bed?" asked Dick.

"Oh, no I don't care for that – if - oh! if mother were but alive," little Tom sobbed aloud.

"I say," said Dick, after a pause. "There's room at my back, if you'll creep in. There! don't be afraid, why, how cold you are, lad."

Dick was sorry for his cousin's loss, but could not speak about it. However, his kind tone sank into Tom's heart, and he fell asleep once more.

The three boys all got up at the same time in the morning, but were not inclined to talk. Jack and Dick put on their clothes as fast as possible, and ran downstairs; but this was quite a different way of going on to what Tom had been accustomed. He looked about for some kind of basin or mug to wash in; there was none not even a jug of water in the room. He slipped on a few necessary clothes, and went downstairs, found a pitcher, and went off to the pump. His cousins, who were playing in the court, laughed at him, and would not tell him where the soap was kept: he had to look some minutes before he could find it. Then he went back to the bedroom; but on entering it from the fresh air, the smell was so oppressive that he could not endure it. Three people had been breathing the air all night, and had used up every particle many times over and over again; and each time that it had been sent out from the lungs, it was less fit than before to be breathed again. They had not felt how poisonous it was while they stayed in it; they had only felt tired and unrefreshed, with a dull headache; but now that Tom came back again into it, he could not mistake its oppressive nature. He went to the window to try and open it. It was what people call a "Yorkshire light," where you know one-half has to be pushed on one side. It was very stiff, for it had not been opened for a long time. Tom pushed against it with all his might; at length it gave way with a jerk; and the shake sent out a cracked pane, which fell on the floor in a hundred little bits. Tom was sadly frightened when he saw what he had done. He would have been sorry to have done mischief at any time, but he had seen enough of his aunt the evening before to find out that she was sharp, and hasty, and cross; and it was hard to have to begin the first day in his new home by getting into a scrape. He sat down on the bedside, and began to cry. But the morning air blowing in upon him, refreshed him, and made him feel stronger. He grew braver as he washed himself in the pure, cold water. "She can't be cross with me longer than a day; by to-night it will be all over; I can bear it for a day."

Dick came running upstairs for something he had forgotten.

"My word, Tom! but you'll catch it!" exclaimed he, when he saw the broken window. He was half pleased at the event, and half sorry for Tom. "Mother did so beat Jack last week for throwing a stone right through the window downstairs. He kept out of the way till night, but she was on the look-out for him, and as soon as she saw him, she caught hold of him and gave it him. Eh! Tom, I would not be you for a deal!"

Tom began to cry again at this account of his aunt's anger; Dick became more and more sorry for him.

"I'll tell thee what; we'll go down and say it was a lad in yon back-yard throwing stones, and that one went smack through the window. I've got one in my pocket that will just do to show."

"No," said Tom, suddenly stopping crying. "I dare not do that."

"Daren't! Why you'll have to dare much more if you go down and face mother without some such story."

"No! I shan't. I shan't have to dare God's anger. Mother taught me to fear that; she said I need never be really afraid of aught else. Just be quiet, Dick, while I say my prayers."

Dick watched his little cousin kneel down by the bed, and bury his face in the clothes; he did not say any set prayer (which Dick was accustomed to think was the only way of praying), but Tom seemed, by the low murmuring which Dick heard, to be talking to a dear friend; and though at first he sobbed and cried, as he asked for help and strength, yet when he got up, his face looked calm and bright, and he spoke quietly as he said to Dick, "Now I'm ready to go and tell aunt."

"Aunt" meanwhile had missed her pitcher and her soap, and was in no good-tempered mood when Tom came to make his confession. She had been hindered in her morning's work by his taking her things away; and now he was come to tell her of the pane being broken and that it must be mended, and money must go all for a child's nonsense.

She gave him (as he had been led to expect) one or two very sharp blows.

Jack and Dick looked on with curiosity, to see how he would take it; Jack, at any rate, expecting a hearty crying from "softy" (Jack himself had cried loudly at his last beating), but Tom never shed a tear, though his face did go very red, and his mouth did grow set with the pain. But what struck the boys more even than his being "hard" in bearing such blows, was his quietness afterwards. He did not grumble loudly, as Jack would have done, nor did he turn sullen, as was Dick's custom; but the minute afterwards he was ready to run an errand for his aunt; nor did he make any mention of the hard blows, when his uncle came in to breakfast, as his aunt had rather expected he would. She was glad he did not, for she knew her husband would have been displeased to know how early she had begun to beat his orphan nephew. So she almost felt grateful to Tom for his silence, and certainly began to be sorry she had struck him so hard.

Poor Tom! he did not know that his cousins were beginning to respect him, nor that his aunt was learning to like him; and he felt very lonely and desolate that first morning. He had nothing to do. Jack went to work at the factory; and Dick went grumbling to school. Tom wondered if he was to go to school again, but he did not like to ask. He sat on a little stool, as much out of his terrible aunt's way as he could. She had her youngest child, a little girl of about a year and a half old, crawling about on the floor. Tom longed to play with her; but he was not sure how far his aunt would like it. But he kept smiling at her, and doing every little thing he could to attract her attention and make her come to him. At last she was coaxed to come upon his knee. His aunt saw it, and though she did not speak, she did not look displeased. He did everything he could think of to amuse little Annie; and her mother was very glad to have her attended to. When Annie grew sleepy, she still kept fast hold of one of Tom's fingers in her little, round, soft hand, and he began to know the happy feeling of loving somebody again.

Only the night before, when his cousins had made him get out of bed, he had wondered if he should live to be an old man, and never have anybody to love all that long time; but now his heart felt quite warm to the little thing that lay on his lap.

"She'll tire you, Tom," said her mother, "you'd better let me put her down in the cot."

"Oh, no!" said he, "please don't! I like so much to have her here." He never moved, though she lay very heavy on his arm, for fear of wakening her.

When she did rouse up, his aunt said, "Thank you, Tom. I've got my work done rarely with you for a nurse. Now take a run in the yard, and play yourself a bit."

His aunt was learning something, and Tom was teaching, though they would both have been very much surprised to hear it. Whenever, in a family, every one is selfish, and (as it is called) "stands up for his own rights," there are no feelings of gratitude; the gracefulness of "thanks" is never called for; nor can there be any occasion for thoughtfulness for others when those others are sure to get the start in thinking for themselves, and taking care of number one. Tom's aunt had never had to remind Jack or Dick to go out to play. They were ready enough to see after their own pleasures.

Well! dinner-time came, and all the family gathered to the meal. It seemed to be a scramble who should be helped first, and cry out for the best pieces. Tom looked very red. His aunt in her new-born liking for him, helped him early to what she thought he would like. But he did not begin to eat. It had been his mother's custom to teach her little son to say a simple "grace" with her before they began their dinner. He expected his uncle to follow the same observance; and waited. Then he felt very hot and shy; but, thinking that it was right to say it, he put away his shyness, and very quietly, but very solemnly said the old accustomed sentence of thanksgiving. Jack burst out laughing when he had done; for which Jack's father gave him a sharp rap and a sharp word, which made him silent through the rest of the dinner. But, excepting Jack, who was angry, I think all the family were the happier for having listened reverently (if with some surprise) to Tom's thanksgiving. They were not an ill-disposed set of people, but wanted thoughtfulness in their every-day life; that sort of thoughtfulness which gives order to a home, and makes a wise and holy spirit of love the groundwork of order.

From that first day Tom never went back in the regard he began then to win. He was useful to his aunt, and patiently bore her hasty ways, until for very shame she left off being hasty with one who was always so meek and mild. His uncle sometimes said he was more like a girl than a boy, as was to be looked for from being brought up for so many years by a woman; but that was the greatest fault he ever had to find with him; and in spite of it, he really respected him for the very qualities which are most truly "manly;" for the courage with which he dared to do what was right, and the quiet firmness with which he bore many kinds of pain. As for little Annie, her friendship and favour and love were the delight of Tom's heart. He did not know how much the others were growing to like him, but Annie showed it in every way, and he loved her in return most dearly. Dick soon found out how useful Tom could be to him in his lessons; for though older than his cousin, Master Dick was a regular dunce, and had never even wished to learn till Tom came; and long before Jack could be brought to acknowledge it, Dick maintained that "Tom had a great deal of pluck in him, though it was not of Jack's kind."

Now I shall jump another year, and tell you a very little about the household twelve months after Tom had entered it. I said above that his aunt had learned to speak less crossly to one who was always gentle after her scoldings. By-and-by her ways to all became less hasty and passionate, for she grew ashamed of speaking to any one in an angry way before Tom; he always looked so sad and sorry to hear her. She has also spoken to him sometimes about his mother; at first because she thought he would like it; but latterly because she became really interested to hear of her ways; and Tom being an only child, and his mother's friend and companion, has been able to tell her of many household arts of comfort, which coming quite unconscious of any purpose, from the lips of a child, have taught her many things which she would have been too proud to learn from an older person. Her husband is softened by the additional cleanliness and peace of his home. He does not now occasionally take refuge in a public-house, to get out of the way of noisy children, an unswept hearth, and a scolding wife. Once when Tom was ill for a day or two, his uncle missed the accustomed grace, and began to say it himself. He is now the person to say "Silence, boys;" and then to ask the blessing on the meal. It makes them gather round the table, instead of sitting down here and there in the comfortless, unsociable way they used to do. Tom and Dick go to school together now, and Dick is getting on famously, and will soon be able to help his next brother over his lessons, as Tom has helped him.

Even Jack has been heard to acknowledge that Tom has "pluck" in him; and as "pluck" in Jack's mind is a short way of summing up all the virtues, he has lately become very fond of his cousin. Tom does not think about happiness, but is happy; and I think we may hope that he, and the household among whom he is adopted, will go "from strength to strength."

Now do you not see how much happier this family are from the one circumstance of a little child's coming among them? Could money have made one-tenth part of this real and increasing happiness? I think you will all say no. And yet Tom was no powerful person; he was not clever; he was very friendless at first; but he was loving and good; and on those two qualities, which any of us may have if we try, the blessing of God lies in rich abundance.

Bessy's Troubles At Home

"Well, mother, I've got you a Southport ticket," said Bessy Lee, as she burst into a room where a pale, sick woman lay dressed on the outside of a bed. "Aren't you glad?" asked she, as her mother moved uneasily, but did not speak.

"Yes, dear, I'm very thankful to you; but your sudden coming in has made my heart flutter so, I'm ready to choke."

Poor Bessy's eyes filled with tears: but, it must be owned, they were tears half of anger. She had taken such pains, ever since the doctor said that Southport was the only thing for her mother, to get her an order from some subscriber to the charity; and she had rushed to her, in the full glow of success, and now her mother seemed more put out by the noise she had made on coming in, than glad to receive the news she had brought.

Mrs. Lee took her hand and tried to speak, but, as she said, she was almost choked with the palpitation at her heart.

"You think it very silly in me, dear, to be so easily startled; but it is not altogether silliness; it is I am so weak that every little noise gives me quite a fright. I shall be better, love, please God, when I come back from Southport. I am so glad you've got the order, for you've taken a deal of pains about it." Mrs. Lee sighed.

"Don't you want to go?" asked Bessy, rather sadly. "You always seem so sorrowful and anxious when we talk about it."

"It's partly my being ailing that makes me anxious, I know," said Mrs.Lee. "But it seems as if so many things might happen while I was away."

Bessy felt a little impatient. Young people in strong health can hardly understand the fears that beset invalids. Bessy was a kind-hearted girl, but rather 'eadstrong, and just now a little disappointed. She forgot that her mother had had to struggle hard with many cares ever since she had been left a widow, and that her illness now had made her nervous.

"What nonsense, mother! What can happen? I can take care of the house and the little ones, and Tom and Jem can take care of themselves. What is to happen?"

"Jenny may fall into the fire," murmured Mrs. Lee, who found little comfort in being talked to in this way. "Or your father's watch may be stolen while you are in, talking with the neighbours, or -"

"Now come, mother, you know I've had the charge of Jenny ever since father died, and you began to go out washing and I'll lock father's watch up in the box in our room."

"Then Tom and Jem won't know at what time to go to the factory. Besides, Bessy," said she, raising herself up, "they're are but young lads, and there's a deal of temptation to take them away from their homes, if their homes are not comfortable and pleasant to them. It's that, more than anything, I've been fretting about all the time I've been ill, that I've lost the power of making this house the cleanest and brightest place they know. But it's no use fretting," said she, falling back weakly upon the bed and sighing. "I must leave it in God's hands. He raiseth up and He bringeth low."

Bessy stood silent for a minute or two. Then she said, "Well, mother, I will try to make home comfortable for the lads, if you'll but keep your mind easy, and go off to Southport quiet and cheerful."

"I'll try," said Mrs. Lee, taking hold of Bessy's hand, and looking up thankfully in her face.

The next Wednesday she set off, leaving home with a heavy heart, which, however, she struggled against, and tried to make more faithful. But she wished her three weeks at Southport were over.

Tom and Jem were both older than Bessy, and she was fifteen. Then came Bill and Mary and little Jenny. They were all good children, and all had faults. Tom and Jem helped to support the family by their earnings at the factory, and gave up their wages very cheerfully for this purpose, to their mother, who, however, insisted on a little being put by every week in the savings' bank. It was one of her griefs now that, when the doctor ordered her some expensive delicacy in the way of diet during her illness (a thing which she persisted in thinking she could have done without), her boys had gone and taken their money out in order to procure it for her. The article in question did not cost one quarter of the amount of their savings, but they had put off returning the remainder into the bank, saying the doctor's bill had yet to be paid, and that it seemed so silly to be always taking money in and out. But meanwhile Mrs. Lee feared lest it should be spent, and begged them to restore it to the savings' bank. This had not been done when she left for Southport. Bill and Mary went to school. Little Jenny was the darling of all, and toddled about at home, having been her sister Bessy's especial charge when all went on well, and the mother used to go out to wash.

Mrs. Lee, however, had always made a point of giving all her children who were at home a comfortable breakfast at seven, before she set out to her day's work; and she prepared the boys' dinner ready for Bessy to warm for them. At night, too, she was anxious to be at home as soon after her boys as she could; and many of her employers respected her wish, and, finding her hard-working and conscientious, took care to set her at liberty early in the evening.

Bessy felt very proud and womanly when she returned home from seeing her mother off by the railway. She looked round the house with a new feeling of proprietorship, and then went to claim little Jenny from the neighbour's where she had been left while Bessy had gone to the station. They asked her to stay and have a bit of chat; but she replied that she could not, for that it was near dinner-time, and she refused the invitation that was then given her to go in some evening. She was full of good plans and resolutions.

That afternoon she took Jenny and went to her teacher's to borrow a book, which she meant to ask one of her brothers to read to her in the evenings while she worked. She knew that it was a book which Jem would like, for though she had never read it, one of her school-fellows had told her it was all about the sea, and desert islands, and cocoanut-trees, just the things that Jem liked to hear about. How happy they would all be this evening.

She hurried Jenny off to bed before her brothers came home; Jenny did not like to go so early, and had to be bribed and coaxed to give up the pleasure of sitting on brother Tom's knee; and when she was in bed, she could not go to sleep, and kept up a little whimper of distress. Bessy kept calling out to her, now in gentle, now in sharp tones, as she made the hearth clean and bright against her brothers' return, as she settled Bill and Mary to their next day's lessons, and got her work ready for a happy evening.

Presently the elder boys came in.

"Where's Jenny?" asked Tom, the first thing.

"I've put her to bed," said Bessy. "I've borrowed a book for you to read to me while I darn the stockings; and it was time for Jenny to go."

"Mother never puts her to bed so soon," said Tom, dissatisfied.

"But she'd be so in the way of any quietness over our reading," said Bessy.

"I don't want to read," said Tom; "I want Jenny to sit on my knee, as she always does, while I eat my supper."

"Tom, Tom, dear Tom!" called out little Jenny, who had heard his voice, and, perhaps, a little of the conversation.

Tom made but two steps upstairs, and re-appeared with Jenny in his arms, in her night-clothes. The little girl looked at Bessy half triumphant and half afraid. Bessy did not speak, but she was evidently very much displeased. Tom began to eat his porridge with Jenny on his knee. Bessy sat in sullen silence; she was vexed with Tom, vexed with Jenny, and vexed with Jem, to gratify whose taste for reading travels she had especially borrowed this book, which he seemed to care so little about. She brooded over her fancied wrongs, ready to fall upon the first person who might give the slightest occasion for anger. It happened to be poor little Jenny, who, by some awkward movement, knocked over the jug of milk, and made a great splash on Bessy's clean white floor.

"Never mind!" said Tom, as Jenny began to cry. "I like my porridge as well without milk as with it."

"Oh, never mind!" said Bessy, her colour rising, and her breath growing shorter. "Never mind dirtying anything, Jenny; it's only giving trouble to Bessy! But I'll make you mind," continued she, as she caught a glance of intelligence peep from Jem's eyes to Tom; and she slapped Jenny's head. The moment she had done it she was sorry for it; she could have beaten herself now with the greatest pleasure for having given way to passion; for she loved little Jenny dearly, and she saw that she really had hurt her. But Jem, with his loud, deep, "For shame, Bessy!" and Tom, with his excess of sympathy with his little sister's wrongs, checked back any expression which Bessy might have uttered of sorrow and regret. She sat there ten times more unhappy than she had been before the accident, hardening her heart to the reproaches of her conscience, yet feeling most keenly that she had been acting wrongly. No one seemed to notice her; this was the evening she had planned and arranged for so busily; and the others, who never thought about it at all, were all quiet and happy, at least in outward appearance, while she was so wretched. By-and-by, she felt the touch of a little soft hand stealing into her own. She looked to see who it was; it was Mary, who till now had been busy learning her lessons, but uncomfortably conscious of the discordant spirit prevailing in the room; and who had at last ventured up to Bessy, as the one who looked the most unhappy, to express, in her own little gentle way, her sympathy in sorrow. Mary was not a quick child; she was plain and awkward in her ways, and did not seem to have many words in which to tell her feelings, but she was very tender and loving, and submitted meekly and humbly to the little slights and rebuffs she often met with for her stupidity.

"Dear Bessy! good night!" said she, kissing her sister; and, at the soft kiss, Bessy's eyes filled with tears, and her heart began to melt.

"Jenny," continued Mary, going to the little spoilt, wilful girl, "will you come to bed with me, and I'll tell you stories about school, and sing you my songs as I undress? Come, little one!" said she, holding out her arms. Jenny was tempted by this speech, and went off to bed in a more reasonable frame of mind than any one had dared to hope.

And now all seemed clear and open for the reading, but each was too proud to propose it. Jem, indeed, seemed to have forgotten the book altogether, he was so busy whittling away at a piece of wood. At last Tom, by a strong effort, said, "Bessy, mayn't we have the book now?"

"No!" said Jem, "don't begin reading, for I must go out and try and make Ned Bates give me a piece of ash-wood, deal is just good for nothing."

"Oh!" said Bessy, "I don't want any one to read this book who does not like it. But I know mother would be better pleased if you were stopping at home quiet, rather than rambling to Ned Bates's at this time of night."

"I know what mother would like as well as you, and I'm not going to be preached to by a girl," said Jem, taking up his cap and going out. Tom yawned and went up to bed. Bessy sat brooding over the evening.

"So much as I thought and I planned! I'm sure I tried to do what was right, and make the boys happy at home. And yet nothing has happened as I wanted it to do. Every one has been so cross and contrary. Tom would take Jenny up when she ought to have been in bed. Jem did not care a straw for this book that I borrowed on purpose for him, but sat laughing. I saw, though he did not think I did, when all was going provoking and vexatious. Mary, no! Mary was a help and a comfort, as she always is, I think, though she is so stupid over her book. Mary always contrives to get people right, and to have her own way somehow; and yet I'm sure she does not take half the trouble I do to please people."

Jem came back soon, disappointed because Ned Bates was out, and could not give him any ash-wood. Bessy said it served him right for going at that time of night, and the brother and sister spoke angrily to each other all the way upstairs, and parted without even saying good-night.

Jenny was asleep when Bessy entered the bedroom which she shared with her sisters and her mother; but she saw Mary's wakeful eyes looking at her as she came in.

"Oh, Mary," said she, "I wish mother was back. The lads would mind her, and now I see they'll just go and get into mischief to spite and plague me."

"I don't think it's for that," said Mary, softly. "Jem did want that ash-wood, I know, for he told me in the morning he didn't think that deal would do. He wants to make a wedge to keep the window from rattling so on windy nights; you know how that fidgets mother."

The next day, little Mary, on her way to school, went round by Ned Bates's to beg a piece of wood for her brother Jem; she brought it home to him at dinner-time, and asked him to be so good as to have everything ready for a quiet whittling at night, while Tom or Bessy read aloud. She told Jenny she would make haste with her lessons, so as to be ready to come to bed early, and talk to her about school (a grand, wonderful place, in Jenny's eyes), and thus Mary quietly and gently prepared for a happy evening, by attending to the kind of happiness for which every one wished.

While Mary had thus been busy preparing for a happy evening, Bessy had been spending part of the afternoon at a Mrs. Foster's, a neighbour of her mother's, and a very tidy, industrious old widow. Mrs. Foster earned part of her livelihood by working for the shops where knitted work of all kinds is to be sold; and Bessy's attention was caught, almost as soon as she went in, by a very gay piece of wool-knitting, in a new stitch, that was to be used as a warm covering for the feet. After admiring its pretty looks, Bessy thought how useful it might be to her mother; and when Mrs. Foster heard this, she offered to teach Bessy how to do it. But where were the wools to come from? Those which Mrs. Foster used were provided her by the shop; and she was a very poor woman - too poor to make presents, though rich enough (as we all are) to give help of many other kinds, and willing too to do what she could (which some of us are not).

The two sat perplexed. "How much did you say it would cost?" said Bessy at last; as if the article was likely to have become cheaper, since she asked the question before.

"Well! it's sure to be more than two shillings if it's German wool. You might get it for eighteenpence if you could be content with English."

"But I've not got eighteenpence," said Bessy, gloomily.

"I could lend it you," said Mrs. Foster, "if I was sure of having it back before Monday. But it's part of my rent-money. Could you make sure, do you think?"

"Oh, yes!" said Bessy, eagerly. "At least I'd try. But perhaps I had better not take it, for after all I don't know where I could get it. What Tom and Jem earn is little enough for the house, now that mother's washing is cut off."

"They are good, dutiful lads, to give it to their mother," said Mrs. Foster, sighing: for she thought of her own boys, that had left her in her old age to toil on, with faded eyesight and weakened strength.

"Oh! but mother makes them each keep a shilling out of it for themselves," said Bessy, in a complaining tone, for she wanted money, and was inclined to envy any one who possessed it.

"That's right enough," said Mrs. Foster. "They that earn it should have some of the power over it."

"But about this wool; this eighteenpence! I wish I was a boy and could earn money. I wish mother would have let me gc to work in the factory."

"Come now, Bessy, I can have none of that nonsense. Thy mother knows what's best for thee; and I'm not going to hear thee complain of what she has thought right. But may be, I can help you to a way of gaining eighteenpence. Mrs. Scott at the worsted shop told me that she should want some one to clean on Saturday; now you're a good strong girl, and can do a woman's work if you've a mind. Shall I say you will go? and then I don't mind if I lend you my eighteenpence. You'll pay me before I want my rent on Monday."

"Oh! thank you, dear Mrs. Foster," said Bessy. "I can scour as well as any woman, mother often says so; and I'll do my best on Saturday; they shan't blame you for having spoken up for me."

"No, Bessy, they won't, I'm sure, if you do your best. You're a good sharp girl for your years."

Bessy lingered for some time, hoping that Mrs. Foster would remember her offer of lending her the money; but finding that she had quite forgotten it, she ventured to remind the kind old woman. That it was nothing but forgetfulness, was evident from the haste with which Mrs. Foster bustled up to her tea-pot and took from it the money required.

"You're as welcome to it as can be, Bessy, as long as I'm sure of its being repaid by Monday. But you're in a mighty hurry about this coverlet," continued she, as she saw Bessy put on her bonnet and prepare to go out.

"Stay, you must take patterns, and go to the right shop in St. Mary's Gate. Why, your mother won't be back this three weeks, child."

"No. But I can't abide waiting, and I want to set to it before it is dark; and you'll teach me the stitch, won't you, when I come back with the wools? I won't be half an hour away."

But Mary and Bill had to "abide waiting" that afternoon; for though the neighbour at whose house the key was left could let them into the house, there was no supper ready for them on their return from school; even Jenny was away spending the afternoon with a playfellow; the fire was nearly out, the milk had been left at a neighbour's; altogether home was very comfortless to the poor tired children, and Bill grumbled terribly; Mary's head ached, and the very tones of her brother's voice, as he complained, gave her pain; and for a minute she felt inclined to sit down and cry. But then she thought of many little sayings which she had heard from her teacher--such as "Never complain of what you can cure," "Bear and forbear," and several other short sentences of a similar description. So she began to make up the fire, and asked Bill to fetch some chips; and when he gave her the gruff answer, that he did not see any use in making a fire when there was nothing to cook by it, she went herself and brought the wood without a word of complaint.

Presently Bill said, "Here! you lend me those bellows; you're not blowing it in the right way; girls never do!" He found out that Mary was wise in making a bright fire ready; for before the blowing was ended, the neighbour with whom the milk had been left brought it in, and little handy Mary prepared the porridge as well as the mother herself could have done. They had just ended when Bessy came in almost breathless; for she had suddenly remembered, in the middle of her knitting-lesson, that Bill and Mary must be at home from school.

"Oh!" she said, "that's right. I have so hurried myself! I was afraid the fire would be out. Where's Jenny? You were to have called for her, you know, as you came from school. Dear! how stupid you are, Mary. I am sure I told you over and over again. Now don't cry, silly child. The best thing you can do is to run off back again for her."

"But my lessons, Bessy. They are so bad to learn. It's tables day to-morrow," pleaded Mary.

"Nonsense; tables are as easy as can be. I can say up to sixteen times sixteen in no time."

"But you know, Bessy, I'm very stupid, and my head aches so to-night!"

"Well! the air will do it good. Really, Mary, I would go myself, only I'm so busy; and you know Bill is too careless, mother says, to fetch Jenny through the streets; and besides they would quarrel, and you can always manage Jenny."

Mary sighed, and went away to bring her sister home. Bessy sat down to her knitting. Presently Bill came up to her with some question about his lesson. She told him the answer without looking at the book; it was all wrong, and made nonsense; but Bill did not care to understand what he learnt, and went on saying, "Twelve inches make one shilling," as contentedly as if it were right.

Mary brought Jenny home quite safely. Indeed, Mary always did succeed in everything, except learning her lessons well; and sometimes, if the teacher could have known how many tasks fell upon the willing, gentle girl at home, she would not have thought that poor Mary was slow or a dunce; and such thoughts would come into the teacher's mind sometimes, although she fully appreciated Mary's sweetness and humility of disposition.

To-night she tried hard at her tables, and all to no use. Her head ached so, she could not remember them, do what she would. She longed to go to her mother, whose cool hands around her forehead always seemed to do her so much good, and whose soft, loving words were such a help to her when she had to bear pain. She had arranged so many plans for to-night, and now all were deranged by Bessy's new fancy for knitting.

But Mary did not see this in the plain, clear light in which I have put it before you. She only was sorry that she could not make haste with her lessons, as she had promised Jenny, who was now upbraiding her with the non-fulfilment of her words. Jenny was still up when Tom and Jem came in. They spoke sharply to Bessy for not having their porridge ready; and while she was defending herself, Mary, even at the risk of imperfect lessons, began to prepare the supper for her brothers. She did it all so quietly, that, almost before they were aware, it was ready for them; and Bessy, suddenly ashamed of herself, and touched by Mary's quiet helpfulness, bent down and kissed her, as once more she settled to the never-ending difficulty of her lesson.

Mary threw her arms round Bessy's neck, and began to cry, for this little mark of affection went to her heart; she had been so longing for a word or a sign of love in her suffering.

"Come, Molly," said Jem, "don't cry like a baby;" but he spoke very kindly. "What's the matter? the old headache come back? Never mind. Go to bed, and it will be better in the morning."

"But I can't go to bed. I don't know my lesson!" Mary looked happier, though the tears were in her eyes.

"I know mine," said Bill, triumphantly.

"Come here," said Jem. "There! I've time enough to whittle away at this before mother comes back. Now let's see this difficult lesson."

Jem's help soon enabled Mary to conquer her lesson; but, meanwhile, Jenny and Bill had taken to quarrelling in spite of Bessy's scolding, administered in small sharp doses, as she looked up from her all-absorbing knitting.

"Well," said Tom, "with this riot on one side, and this dull lesson on the other, and Bessy as cross as can be in the midst, I can understand what makes a man go out to spend his evenings from home."

Bessy looked up, suddenly wakened up to a sense of the danger which her mother had dreaded.

Bessy thought it was very fortunate that it fell on a Saturday, of all days in the week, that Mrs. Scott wanted her; for Mary would be at home, who could attend to the household wants of everybody; and so she satisfied her conscience at leaving the post of duty that her mother had assigned to her, and that she had promised to fulfil. She was so eager about her own plans that she did not consider this; she did not consider at all, or else I think she would have seen many things to which she seemed to be blind now. When were Mary's lessons for Monday to be learnt? Bessy knew as well as we do, that lesson-learning was hard work to Mary. If Mary worked as hard as she could after morning school she could hardly get the house cleaned up bright and comfortable before her brothers came home from the factory, which "loosed" early on the Saturday afternoon; and if pails of water, chairs heaped up one on the other, and tables put topsy-turvy on the dresser, were the most prominent objects in the house-place, there would be no temptation for the lads to stay at home; besides which, Mary, tired and weary (however gentle she might be), would not be able to give the life to the evening that Bessy, a clever, spirited girl, near their own age, could easily do, if she chose to be interested and sympathising in what they had to tell. But Bessy did not think of all this. What she did think about was the pleasant surprise she should give her mother by the warm and pretty covering for her feet, which she hoped to present her with on her return home. And if she had done the duties she was pledged to on her mother's departure first, if they had been compatible with her plan of being a whole day absent from home, in order to earn the money for the wools, the project of the surprise would have been innocent and praiseworthy.

Bessy prepared everything for dinner before she left home that Saturday morning. She made a potato-pie all ready for putting in the oven; she was very particular in telling Mary what was to be cleaned, and how it was all to be cleaned; and then she kissed the children, and ran off to Mrs. Scott's. Mary was rather afraid of the responsibility thrust upon her; but still she was pleased that Bessy could trust her to do so much. She took Jenny to the ever-useful neighbour, as she and Bill went to school; but she was rather frightened when Mrs. Jones began to grumble about these frequent visits of the child.

"I was ready enough to take care of the wench when thy mother was ill; there was reason for that. And the child is a nice child enough, when she is not cross; but still there are some folks, it seems, who, if you give them an inch, will take an ell. Where's Bessy, that she can't mind her own sister?"

"Gone out charing," said Mary, clasping the little hand in hers tighter, for she was afraid of Mrs. Jones's anger.

"I could go out charing every day in the week if I'd the face to trouble other folks with my children," said Mrs. Jones, in a surly tone.

"Shall I take her back, ma'am?" said Mary, timidly, though she knew this would involve her staying away from school, and being blamed by the dear teacher. But Mrs. Jones growled worse than she bit, this time at least.

"No," said she, "you may leave her with me. I suppose she's had her breakfast?"

"Yes; and I'll fetch her away as soon as ever I can after twelve."

If Mary had been one to consider the hardships of her little lot, she might have felt this morning's occurrence as one; that she, who dreaded giving trouble to anybody, and was painfully averse from asking any little favour for herself, should be the very one on whom it fell to presume upon another person's kindness. But Mary never did think of any hardships; they seemed the natural events of life, and as if it was fitting and proper that she, who managed things badly, and was such a dunce, should be blamed. Still she was rather flurried by Mrs. Jones's scolding; and almost wished that she had taken Jenny home again. Her lessons were not well said, owing to the distraction of her mind.

When she went for Jenny she found that Mrs. Jones, repenting of her sharp words, had given the little girl bread and treacle, and made her very comfortable; so much so that Jenny was not all at once ready to leave her little playmates, and when once she had set out on the road, she was in no humour to make haste. Mary thought of the potato-pie and her brothers, and could almost have cried, as Jenny, heedless of her sister's entreaties, would linger at the picture-shops.

"I shall be obliged to go and leave you, Jenny! I must get dinner ready."

"I don't care," said Jenny. "I don't want any dinner, and I can come home quite well by myself."

Mary half longed to give her a fright, it was so provoking. But she thought of her mother, who was so anxious always about Jenny, and she did not do it. She kept patiently trying to attract her onwards, and at last they were at home. Mary stirred up the fire, which was to all appearance quite black; it blazed up, but the oven was cold. She put the pie in, and blew the fire; but the paste was quite white and soft when her brothers came home, eager and hungry.

"Oh! Mary, what a manager you are!" said Tom. "Any one else would have remembered and put the pie in in time."

Mary's eyes filled full of tears; but she did not try to justify herself. She went on blowing, till Jem took the bellows, and kindly told her to take off her bonnet, and lay the cloth. Jem was always kind. He gave Tom the best baked side of the pie, and quietly took the side himself where the paste was little better than dough, and the potatoes quite hard; and when he caught Mary's little anxious face watching him, as he had to leave part of his dinner untasted, he said, "Mary, I should like this pie warmed up for supper; there is nothing so good as potato-pie made hot the second time."

Tom went off saying, "Mary, I would not have you for a wife on any account. Why, my dinner would never be ready, and your sad face would take away my appetite if it were."

But Jem kissed her and said, "Never mind, Mary! you and I will live together, old maid and old bachelor."

So she could set to with spirit to her cleaning, thinking there never was such a good brother as Jem; and as she dwelt upon his perfections, she thought who it was who had given her such a good, kind brother, and felt her heart full of gratitude to Him. She scoured and cleaned in right-down earnest. Jenny helped her for some time, delighted to be allowed to touch and lift things. But then she grew tired; and Bill was out of doors; so Mary had to do all by herself, and grew very nervous and frightened, lest all should not be finished and tidy against Tom came home. And the more frightened she grew, the worse she got on. Her hands trembled, and things slipped out of them; and she shook so, she could not lift heavy pieces of furniture quickly and sharply; and in the middle the clock struck the hour for her brothers' return, when all ought to have been tidy and ready for tea. She gave it up in despair, and began to cry.

"Oh, Bessy, Bessy! why did you go away? I have tried hard, and I cannot do it," said she aloud, as if Bessy could hear.

"Dear Mary, don't cry," said Jenny, suddenly coming away from her play. "I'll help you. I am very strong. I can do anything. I can lift that pan off the fire."

The pan was full of boiling water, ready for Mary. Jenny took hold of the handle, and dragged it along the bar over the fire. Mary sprung forwards in terror to stop the little girl. She never knew how it was, but the next moment her arm and side were full of burning pain, which turned her sick and dizzy, and Jenny was crying passionately beside her.

"Oh, Mary! Mary! Mary! my hand is so scalded. What shall I do? I cannot bear it. It's all about my feet on the ground." She kept shaking her hand to cool it by the action of the air. Mary thought that she herself was dying, so acute and terrible was the pain; she could hardly keep from screaming out aloud; but she felt that if she once began she could not stop herself, so she sat still, moaning, and the tears running down her face like rain. "Go, Jenny," said she, "and tell some one to come."

"I can't, I can't, my hand hurts so," said Jenny. But she flew wildly out of the house the next minute, crying out, "Mary is dead. Come, come, come!" For Mary could bear it no longer; but had fainted away, and looked, indeed, like one that was dead. Neighbours flocked in; and one ran for a doctor. In five minutes Tom and Jem came home. What a home it seems! People they hardly knew standing in the house-place, which looked as if it had never been cleaned--all was so wet, and in such disorder, and dirty with the trampling of many feet; Jenny still crying passionately, but half comforted at being at present the only authority as to how the affair happened; and faint moans from the room upstairs, where some women were cutting the clothes off poor Mary, preparatory for the doctor's inspection. Jem said directly, "Some one go straight to Mrs. Scott's, and fetch our Bessy. Her place is here, with Mary."

And then he civilly, but quietly, dismissed all the unnecessary and useless people, feeling sure that in case of any kind of illness, quiet was the best thing. Then he went upstairs.

Mary's face was scarlet now with violent pain; but she smiled a little through her tears at seeing Jem. As for him, he cried outright.

"I don't think it was anybody's fault, Jem," said she, softly. "It was very heavy to lift."

"Are you in great pain, dear?" asked Jem, in a whisper.

"I think I'm killed, Jem. I do think I am. And I did so want to see mother again."

"Nonsense!" said the woman who had been helping Mary. For, as she said afterwards, whether Mary died or lived, crying was a bad thing for her; and she saw the girl was ready to cry when she thought of her mother, though she had borne up bravely all the time the clothes were cut off.

Bessy's face, which had been red with hard running, faded to a dead white when she saw Mary; she looked so shocked and ill that Jem had not the heart to blame her, although the minute before she came in, he had been feeling very angry with her. Bessy stood quite still at the foot of Mary's bed, never speaking a word, while the doctor examined her side and felt her pulse; only great round tears gathered in her eyes, and rolled down her cheeks, as she saw Mary quiver with pain. Jem followed the doctor downstairs. Then Bessy went and knelt beside Mary, and wiped away the tears that were trickling down the little face.

"Is it very bad, Mary?" asked Bessy.

"Oh yes! yes! if I speak, I shall scream."

Then Bessy covered her head in the bed-clothes and cried outright.

"I was not cross, was I? I did not mean to be but I hardly know what I am saying," moaned out little Mary. "Please forgive me, Bessy, if I was cross."

"God forgive me!" said Bessy, very low. They were the first words she had spoken since she came home. But there could be no more talking between the sisters, for now the woman returned who had at first been assisting Mary. Presently Jem came to the door, and beckoned. Bessy rose up, and went with, him below. Jem looked very grave, yet not so sad as he had done before the doctor came. "He says she must go into the infirmary. He will see about getting her in."

"Oh, Jem! I did so want to nurse her myself!" said Bessy, imploringly. "It was all my own fault," (she choked with crying); "and I thought I might do that for her, to make up."

"My dear Bessy,"before he had seen Bessy, he had thought he could never call her "dear" again, but now he began "My dear Bessy, we both want Mary to get better, don't we? I am sure we do. And we want to take the best way of making her so, whatever that is; well, then, I think we must not be considering what we should like best just for ourselves, but what people, who know as well as doctors do, say is the right way. I can't remember all that he said; but I'm clear that he told me, all wounds on the skin required more and better air to heal in than Mary could have here: and there the doctor will see her twice a day, if need be."

Bessy shook her head, but could not speak at first. At last she said, "Jem, I did so want to do something for her. No one could nurse her as I should."

Jem was silent. At last he took Bessy's hand, for he wanted to say something to her that he was afraid might vex her, and yet that he thought he ought to say.

"Bessy!" said he, "when mother went away, you planned to do all things right at home, and to make us all happy. I know you did. Now may I tell you how I think you went wrong? Don't be angry, Bessy."

"I think I shall never have spirit enough in me to be angry again," said Bessy, humbly and sadly.

"So much the better, dear. But don't over-fret about Mary. The doctor has good hopes of her, if he can get her into the infirmary. Now, I'm going on to tell you how I think you got wrong after mother left. You see, Bessy, you wanted to make us all happy your way--as you liked; just as you are wanting now to nurse Mary in your way, and as you like. Now, as far as I can make out, those folks who make home the happiest, are people who try and find out how others think they could be happy, and then, if it's not wrong, help them on with their wishes as far as they can. You know, you wanted us all to listen to your book; and very kind it was in you to think of it; only, you see, one wanted to whittle, and another wanted to do this or that, and then you were vexed with us all. I don't say but what I should have been if I had been in your place, and planned such a deal for others; only lookers-on always see a deal; and I saw that if you'd done what poor little Mary did next day, we should all have been far happier. She thought how she could forward us in our plans, instead of trying to force a plan of her own on us. She got me my right sort of wood for whittling, and arranged all nicely to get the little ones off to bed, so as to get the house quiet, if you wanted some reading, as she thought you did. And that's the way, I notice, some folks have of making a happy home. Others may mean just as well, but they don't hit the thing."

"I dare say it's true," said Bessy. "But sometimes you all hang about as if you did not know what to do. And I thought reading travels would just please you all."

Jem was touched by Bessy's humble way of speaking, so different from her usual cheerful, self-confident manner. He answered, "I know you did, dear. And many a time we should have been glad enough of it, when we had nothing to do, as you say."

"I had promised mother to try and make you all happy, and this is the end of it!" said Bessy, beginning to cry afresh.

"But, Bessy! I think you were not thinking of your promise, when you fixed to go out and char."

"I thought of earning money."

"Earning money would not make us happy. We have enough, with care and management. If you were to have made us happy, you should have been at home, with a bright face, ready to welcome us; don't you think so, dear Bessy?"

"I did not want the money for home. I wanted to make mother a present of such a pretty thing!"

"Poor mother! I am afraid we must send for her home now. And she has only been three days at Southport!"

"Oh!" said Bessy, startled by this notion of Jem's; "don't, don't send for mother. The doctor did say so much about her going to Southport being the only thing for her, and I did so try to get her an order! It will kill her, Jem! indeed it will; you don't know how weak and frightened she is, oh, Jem, Jem!"

Jem felt the truth of what his sister was saying. At last, he resolved to leave the matter for the doctor to decide, as he had attended his mother, and now knew exactly how much danger there was about Mary. He proposed to Bessy that they should go and relieve the kind neighbour who had charge of Mary.

"But you won't send for mother," pleaded Bessy; "if it's the best thing for Mary, I'll wash up her things to-night, all ready for her to go into the infirmary. I won't think of myself, Jem."

"Well! I must speak to the doctor," said Jem. "I must not try and fix any way just because we wish it, but because it is right."

All night long, Bessy washed and ironed, and yet was always ready to attend to Mary when Jem called her. She took Jenny's scalded hand in charge as well, and bathed it with the lotion the doctor sent; and all was done so meekly and patiently that even Tom was struck with it, and admired the change. The doctor came very early. He had prepared everything for Mary's admission into the infirmary. And Jem consulted him about sending for his mother home. Bessy sat trembling, awaiting his answer.

"I am very unwilling to sanction any concealment. And yet, as you say, your mother is in a very delicate state. It might do her serious harm if she had any shock. Well! suppose for this once, I take it on myself. If Mary goes on as I hope, why, well! well! we'll see. Mind that your mother is told all when she comes home. And if our poor Mary grows worse but I'm not afraid of that, with infirmary care and nursing but if she does, I'll write to your mother myself, and arrange with a kind friend I have at Southport all about sending her home. And now," said he, turning suddenly to Bessy, "tell me what you were doing from home when this happened. Did not your mother leave you in charge of all at home?"

"Yes, sir!" said Bessy, trembling. "But, sir, I thought I could earn money to make mother a present!"

"Thought! fiddle-de-dee. I'll tell you what; never you neglect the work clearly laid out for you by either God or man, to go making work for yourself, according to your own fancies. God knows what you are most fit for. Do that. And then wait; if you don't see your next duty clearly. You will not long be idle in this world, if you are ready for a summons. Now let me see that you send Mary all clean and tidy to the infirmary."

Jem was holding Bessy's hand. "She has washed everything and made it fit for a queen. Our Bessy worked all night long, and was content to let me be with Mary (where she wished sore to be), because I could lift her better, being the stronger."

"That's right. Even when you want to be of service to others, don't think how to please yourself."

I have not much more to tell you about Bessy. This sad accident of Mary's did her a great deal of good, although it cost her so much sorrow at first. It taught her several lessons, which it is good for every woman to learn, whether she is called upon, as daughter, sister, wife, or mother, to contribute to the happiness of a home. And Mary herself was hardly more thoughtful and careful to make others happy in their own way, provided that way was innocent, than was Bessy hereafter. It was a struggle between her and Mary which could be the least selfish, and do the duties nearest to them with the most faithfulness and zeal. The mother stayed at Southport her full time, and came home well and strong. Then Bessy put her arms round her mother's neck, and told her all--and far more severely against herself than either the doctor or Jem did, when they related the same story afterwards.

Disappearances

I am not in the habit of seeing the Household Words regularly; but a friend, who lately sent me some of the back numbers, recommended me to read "all the papers relating to the Detective and Protective Police," which I accordingly did not as the generality of readers have done, as they appeared week by week, or with pauses between, but consecutively, as a popular history of the Metropolitan Police; and, as I suppose it may also be considered, a history of the police force in every large town in England. When I had ended these papers, I did not feel disposed to read any others at that time, but preferred falling into a train of reverie and recollection.

First of all I remembered, with a smile, the unexpected manner in which a relation of mine was discovered by an acquaintance, who had mislaid or forgotten Mr. B.'s address. Now my dear cousin, Mr. B., charming as he is in many points, has the little peculiarity of liking to change his lodgings once every three months on an average, which occasions some bewilderment to his country friends, who have no sooner learnt the 19, Belle Vue Road, Hampstead, than they have to take pains to forget that address, and to remember the 27½, Upper Brown Street, Camberwell; and so on, till I would rather learn a page of Walker's Pronouncing Dictionary, than try to remember the variety of directions which I have had to put on my letters to Mr. B. during the last three years. Last summer it pleased him to remove to a beautiful village not ten miles out of London, where there is a railway station. Thither his friend sought him. (I do not now speak of the following scent there had been through three or four different lodgings, where Mr. B. had been residing, before his country friend ascertained that he was now lodging at R----.) He spent the morning in making inquiries as to Mr. B.'s whereabouts in the village; but many gentlemen were lodging there for the summer, and neither butcher nor baker could inform him where Mr. B. was staying; his letters were unknown at the post-office, which was accounted for by the circumstance of their always being directed to his office in town. At last the country friend sauntered back to the railway-office, and while he waited for the train he made inquiry, as a last resource, of the book-keeper at the station. "No, sir, I cannot tell you where Mr. B. lodges--so many gentlemen go by the trains; but I have no doubt but that the person standing by that pillar can inform you." The individual to whom he directed the inquirer's attention had the appearance of a tradesman, respectable enough, yet with no pretensions to "gentility," and had, apparently, no more urgent employment than lazily watching the passengers who came dropping in to the station. However, when he was spoken to, he answered civilly and promptly. "Mr. B.? tall gentleman, with light hair? Yes, sir, I know Mr. B. He lodges at No. 8, Morton Villas--has done these three weeks or more; but you'll not find him there, sir, now. He went to town by the eleven o'clock train, and does not usually return until the half-past four train."

The country friend had no time to lose in returning to the village, to ascertain the truth of this statement. He thanked his informant, and said he would call on Mr. B. at his office in town; but before he left R----station, he asked the book-keeper who the person was to whom he had referred him for information as to his friend's place of residence. "One of the Detective Police, sir," was the answer. I need hardly say that Mr. B., not without a little surprise, confirmed the accuracy of the policeman's report in every particular.

When I heard this anecdote of my cousin and his friend, I thought that there could be no more romances written on the same kind of plot as Caleb Williams; the principal interest of which, to the superficial reader, consists in the alternation of hope and fear, that the hero may, or may not, escape his pursuer. It is long since I have read the story, and I forget the name of the offended and injured gentleman, whose privacy Caleb has invaded; but I know that his pursuit of Caleb, his detection of the various hiding-places of the latter his following up of slight clues all, in fact, depended upon his own energy, sagacity, and perseverance. The interest was caused by the struggle of man against man; and the uncertainty as to which would ultimately be successful in his object; the unrelenting pursuer, or the ingenious Caleb, who seeks by every device to conceal himself. Now, in 1851, the offended master would set the Detective Police to work; there would be no doubt as to their success; the only question would be as to the time that would elapse before the hiding-place could be detected, and that could not be a question long. It is no longer a struggle between man and man, but between a vast organized machinery, and a weak, solitary individual; we have no hopes, no fears, only certainty. But if the materials of pursuit and evasion, as long as the chase is confined to England, are taken away from the store-house of the romancer, at any rate we can no more be haunted by the idea of the possibility of mysterious disappearances; and any one who has associated much with those who were alive at the end of the last century, can testify that there was some reason for such fears.

When I was a child, I was sometimes permitted to accompany a relation to drink tea with a very clever old lady, of one hundred and twenty or, so I thought then; I now think she, perhaps, was only about seventy. She was lively, and intelligent, and had seen and known much that was worth narrating. She was a cousin of the Sneyds, the family whence Mr. Edgeworth took two of his wives; had known Major André; had mixed in the Old Whig Society that the beautiful Duchess of Devonshire and "Buff and Blue Mrs. Crewe" gathered round them; her father had been one of the early patrons of the lovely Miss Linley. I name these facts to show that she was too intelligent and cultivated by association, as well as by natural powers, to lend an over-easy credence to the marvellous; and yet I have heard her relate stories of disappearances which haunted my imagination longer than any tale of wonder. One of her stories was this: Her father's estate lay in Shropshire, and his park-gates opened right on to a scattered village of which he was landlord. The houses formed a straggling irregular street here a garden, next a gable-end of a farm, there a row of cottages, and so on. Now, at the end house or cottage lived a very respectable man and his wife. They were well known in the village, and were esteemed for the patient attention which they paid to the husband's father, a paralytic old man. In winter, his chair was near the fire; in summer, they carried him out into the open space in front of the house to bask in the sunshine, and to receive what placid amusement he could from watching the little passings to and fro of the villagers. He could not move from his bed to his chair without help. One hot and sultry June day, all the village turned out to the hay-fields. Only the very old and the very young remained.

The old father of whom I have spoken was carried out to bask in the sunshine that afternoon as usual, and his son and daughter-in-law went to the hay-making. But when they came home in the early evening, their paralysed father had disappeared, was gone! and from that day forwards, nothing more was ever heard of him. The old lady, who told this story, said with the quietness that always marked the simplicity of her narration, that every inquiry which her father could make was made, and that it could never be accounted for. No one had observed any stranger in the village; no small household robbery, to which the old man might have been supposed an obstacle, had been committed in his son's dwelling that afternoon. The son and daughter-in-law (noted too for their attention to the helpless father) had been a-field among all the neighbours the whole of the time. In short, it never was accounted for; and left a painful impression on many minds.

I will answer for it, the Detective Police would have ascertained every fact relating to it in a week.

This story from its mystery was painful, but had no consequences to make it tragical. The next which I shall tell (and although traditionary, these anecdotes of disappearances which I relate in this paper are correctly repeated, and were believed by my informants to be strictly true), had consequences, and melancholy ones too. The scene of it is in a little country-town, surrounded by the estates of several gentlemen of large property. About a hundred years ago there lived in this small town an attorney, with his mother and sister. He was agent for one of the squires near, and received rents for him on stated days, which of course were well known. He went at these times to a small public-house, perhaps five miles from ----, where the tenants met him, paid their rents, and were entertained at dinner afterwards. One night he did not return from this festivity. He never returned. The gentleman whose agent he was, employed the Dogberrys of the time to find him, and the missing cash; the mother, whose support and comfort he was, sought him with all the perseverance of faithful love. But he never returned; and by-and-by the rumour spread that he must have gone abroad with the money; his mother heard the whispers all around her, and could not disprove it; and so her heart broke, and she died. Years after, I think as many as fifty, the well-to-do butcher and grazier of ---- died; but, before his death, he confessed that he had waylaid Mr. ---- on the heath close to the town, almost within call of his own house, intending only to rob him, but meeting with more resistance than he anticipated, had been provoked to stab him; and had buried him that very night deep under the loose sand of the heath. There his skeleton was found; but too late for his poor mother to know that his fame was cleared. His sister, too, was dead, unmarried, for no one liked the possibilities which might arise from being connected with the family. None cared if he was guilty or innocent now.

If our Detective Police had only been in existence!

This last is hardly a story of unaccounted-for disappearance. It is only unaccounted for in one generation. But disappearances never to be accounted for on any supposition are not uncommon, among the traditions of the last century. I have heard (and I think I have read it in one of the earlier numbers of Chambers's Journal), of a marriage which took place in Lincolnshire about the year 1750. It was not then de rigueur that the happy couple should set out on a wedding journey; but instead, they and their friends had a merry jovial dinner at the house of either bride or groom; and in this instance the whole party adjourned to the bridegroom's residence, and dispersed, some to ramble in the garden, some to rest in the house until the dinner-hour. The bridegroom, it is to be supposed, was with his bride, when he was suddenly summoned away by a domestic, who said that a stranger wished to speak to him; and henceforward he was never seen more. The same tradition hangs about an old deserted Welsh Hall standing in a wood near Festiniog; there, too, the bridegroom was sent for to give audience to a stranger on his wedding-day, and disappeared from the face of the earth from that time; but there, they tell in addition, that the bride lived long, that she passed her three-score years and ten, but that daily during all those years, while there was light of sun or moon to lighten the earth, she sat watching, watching at one particular window which commanded a view of the approach to the house. Her whole faculties, her whole mental powers, became absorbed in that weary watching; long before she died, she was childish, and only conscious of one wish to sit in that long high window, and watch the road, along which he might come. She was as faithful as Evangeline, if pensive and inglorious.

That these two similar stories of disappearance on a wedding-day "obtained," as the French say, shows us that anything which adds to our facility of communication, and organization of means, adds to our security of life. Only let a bridegroom try to disappear from an untamed Katherine of a bride, and he will soon be brought home, like a recreant coward, overtaken by the electric telegraph, and clutched back to his fate by a detective policeman.

Two more stories of disappearance, and I have done. I will give you the last in date first, because it is the most melancholy; and we will wind up cheerfully (after a fashion). Some time between 1820 and 1830, there lived in North Shields a respectable old woman, and her son, who was trying to struggle into sufficient knowledge of medicine, to go out as ship-surgeon in a Baltic vessel, and perhaps in this manner to earn money enough to spend a session in Edinburgh. He was furthered in all his plans by the late benevolent Dr. G----, of that town. I believe the usual premium was not required in his case; the young man did many useful errands and offices which a finer young gentleman would have considered beneath him; and he resided with his mother in one of the alleys (or "chares,") which lead down from the main street of North Shields to the river. Dr. G----had been with a patient all night, and left her very early on a winter's morning to return home to bed; but first he stepped down to his apprentice's home, and bade him get up, and follow him to his own house, where some medicine was to be mixed, and then taken to the lady. Accordingly the poor lad came, prepared the dose, and set off with it some time between five and six on a winter's morning. He was never seen again. Dr. G---- waited, thinking he was at his mother's house; she waited, considering that he had gone to his day's work. And meanwhile, as people remembered afterwards, the small vessel bound to Edinburgh sailed out of port. The mother expected him back her whole life long; but some years afterwards occurred the discoveries of the Hare and Burke horrors, and people seemed to gain a dark glimpse at his fate; but I never heard that it was fully ascertained, or indeed more than surmised. I ought to add that all who knew him spoke emphatically as to his steadiness of purpose, and conduct, so as to render it improbable in the highest degree that he had run off to sea, or suddenly changed his plan of life in any way.

My last story is one of a disappearance which was accounted for after many years. There is a considerable street in Manchester leading from the centre of the town to some of the suburbs. This street is called at one part Garratt, and afterwards, where it emerges into gentility and, comparatively, country, Brook Street. It derives its former name from an old black-and-white hall of the time of Richard the Third, or thereabouts, to judge from the style of building; they have closed in what is left of the old hall now; but a few years since this old house was visible from the main road; it stood low on some vacant ground, and appeared to be half in ruins. I believe it was occupied by several poor families who rented tenements in the tumble-down dwelling. But formerly it was Gerard Hall, (what a difference between Gerard and Garratt!) and was surrounded by a park with a clear brook running through it, with pleasant fish-ponds, (the name of these was preserved until very lately, on a street near,) orchards, dovecotes, and similar appurtenances to the manor-houses of former days. I am almost sure that the family to whom it belonged were Mosleys, probably a branch of the tree of the lord of the Manor of Manchester. Any topographical work of the last century relating to their district would give the name of the last proprietor of the old stock, and it is to him that my story refers.

Many years ago there lived in Manchester two old maiden ladies, of high respectability. All their lives had been spent in the town, and they were fond of relating the changes which had taken place within their recollection, which extended back to seventy or eighty years from the present time. They knew much of its traditionary history from their father, as well; who, with his father before him, had been respectable attorneys in Manchester, during the greater part of the last century: they were, also, agents for several of the county families, who, driven from their old possessions by the enlargement of the town, found some compensation in the increased value of any land which they might choose to sell. Consequently the Messrs. S----, father and son, were conveyancers in good repute, and acquainted with several secret pieces of family history, one of which related to Garratt Hall.

The owner of this estate, some time in the first half of the last century, married young; he and his wife had several children, and lived together in a quiet state of happiness for many years. At last, business of some kind took the husband up to London; a week's journey in those days. He wrote and announced his arrival; I do not think he ever wrote again. He seemed to be swallowed up in the abyss of the metropolis, for no friend (and the lady had many and powerful friends) could ever ascertain for her what had become of him; the prevalent idea was that he had been attacked by some of the street-robbers who prowled about in those days, that he had resisted, and had been murdered. His wife gradually gave up all hopes of seeing him again, and devoted herself to the care of her children; and so they went on, tranquilly enough, until the heir came of age, when certain deeds were necessary before he could legally take possession of the property. These deeds Mr. S---- (the family lawyer) stated had been given up by him into the missing gentleman's keeping just before the last mysterious journey to London, with which I think they were in some way concerned. It was possible that they were still in existence; some one in London might have them in possession, and be either conscious or unconscious of their importance. At any rate, Mr. S----'s advice to his client was that he should put an advertisement in the London papers, worded so skilfully that any one who might hold the important documents should understand to what it referred, and no one else. This was accordingly done; and although repeated at intervals for some time, it met with no success. But at last a mysterious answer was sent; to the effect that the deeds were in existence, and should be given up; but only on certain conditions, and to the heir himself. The young man, in consequence, went up to London, and adjourned, according to directions, to an old house in Barbican, where he was told by a man, apparently awaiting him, that he must submit to be blindfolded, and must follow his guidance. He was taken through several long passages before he left the house; at the termination of one of these he was put into a sedan-chair, and carried about for an hour or more; he always reported that there were many turnings, and that he imagined he was set down finally not very far from his starting point.

When his eyes were unbandaged, he was in a decent sitting-room, with tokens of family occupation lying about. A middle-aged gentleman entered, and told him that, until a certain time had elapsed (which should be indicated to him in a particular way, but of which the length was not then named), he must swear to secrecy as to the means by which he obtained possession of the deeds. This oath was taken; and then the gentleman, not without some emotion, acknowledged himself to be the missing father of the heir. It seems that he had fallen in love with a damsel, a friend of the person with whom he lodged. To this young woman he had represented himself as unmarried; she listened willingly to his wooing, and her father, who was a shopkeeper in the City, was not averse to the match, as the Lancashire squire had a goodly presence, and many similar qualities, which the shopkeeper thought might be acceptable to his customers. The bargain was struck; the descendant of a knightly race married the only daughter of the City shopkeeper, and became a junior partner in the business. He told his son that he had never repented the step he had taken; that his lowly-born wife was sweet, docile, and affectionate; that his family by her was large; and that he and they were thriving and happy. He inquired after his first (or rather, I should say, his true) wife with friendly affection; approved of what she had done with regard to his estate, and the education of his children; but said that he considered he was dead to her, as she was to him. When he really died he promised that a particular message, the nature of which he specified, should be sent to his son at Garrett; until then they would not hear more of each other; for it was of no use attempting to trace him under his incognito, even if the oath did not render such an attempt forbidden. I dare say the youth had no great desire to trace out the father, who had been one in name only. He returned to Lancashire; took possession of the property at Manchester; and many years elapsed before he received the mysterious intimation of his father's real death. After that, he named the particulars connected with the recovery of the title-deeds to Mr. S., and one or two intimate friends. When the family became extinct, or removed from Garratt, it became no longer any very closely kept secret, and I was told the tale of the disappearance by Miss S., the aged daughter of the family agent.

Once more, let me say I am thankful I live in the days of the Detective Police; if I am murdered, or commit bigamy, at any rate my friends will have the comfort of knowing all about it.

A correspondent has favoured us with the sequel of the disappearance of the pupil of Dr. G., who vanished from North Shields, in charge of certain potions he was entrusted with, very early one morning, to convey to a patient: "Dr. G.'s son married my sister, and the young man who disappeared was a pupil in the house. When he went out with the medicine, he was hardly dressed, having merely thrown on some clothes; and he went in slippers, which incidents induced the belief that he was made away with. After some months his family put on mourning; and the G.'s (very timid people) were so sure that he was murdered, that they wrote verses to his memory, and became sadly worn by terror. But, after a long time (I fancy, but am not sure, about a year and a half), came a letter from the young man, who was doing well in America. His explanation was, that a vessel was lying at the wharf about to sail in the morning, and the youth, who had long meditated evasion, thought it a good opportunity, and stepped on board, after leaving the medicine at the proper door. I spent some weeks at Dr. G.'s after the occurrence; and very doleful we used to be about it. But the next time I went they were, naturally, very angry with the inconsiderate young man."

Right At Last

Doctor Brown was poor, and had to make his way in the world. He had gone to study his profession in Edinburgh, and his energy, ability, and good conduct had entitled him to some notice on the part of the professors. Once introduced to the ladies of their families, his prepossessing appearance and pleasing manners made him a universal favourite; and perhaps no other student received so many invitations to dancing- and evening-parties, or was so often singled out to fill up an odd vacancy at the last moment at the dinner-table. No one knew particularly who he was, or where he sprang from; but then he had no near relations, as he had once or twice observed; so he was evidently not hampered with low-born or low-bred connections. He had been in mourning for his mother, when he first came to college.

All this much was recalled to the recollection of Professor Frazer by his niece Margaret, as she stood before him one morning in his study; telling him, in a low, but resolute voice that, the night before, Doctor James Brown had offered her marriage - that she had accepted him - and that he was intending to call on Professor Frazer (her uncle and natural guardian) that very morning, to obtain his consent to their engagement. Professor Frazer was perfectly aware, from Margaret's manner, that his consent was regarded by her as a mere form, for that her mind was made up: and he had more than once had occasion to find out how inflexible she could be. Yet he, too, was of the same blood, and held to his own opinions in the same obdurate manner. The consequence of which frequently was, that uncle and niece had argued themselves into mutual bitterness of feeling, without altering each other's opinions one jot. But Professor Frazer could not restrain himself on this occasion, of all others.

"Then, Margaret, you will just quietly settle down to be a beggar, for that lad Brown has little or no money to think of marrying upon: you that might be my Lady Kennedy, if you would!"

"I could not, uncle."

"Nonsense, child! Sir Alexander is a personable and agreeable man, middle-aged, if you will, well, a wilful woman maun have her way; but, if I had had a notion that this youngster was sneaking into my house to cajole you into fancying him, I would have seen him far enough before I had ever let your aunt invite him to dinner. Ay! you may mutter; but I say, no gentleman would ever have come into my house to seduce my niece's affections, without first informing me of his intentions, and asking my leave."

"Doctor Brown is a gentleman, Uncle Frazer, whatever you may think of him."

"So you think, so you think. But who cares for the opinion of a love-sick girl? He is a handsome, plausible young fellow, of good address. And I don't mean to deny his ability. But there is something about him I never did like, and now it's accounted for. And Sir Alexander ---- Well, well! your aunt will be disappointed in you, Margaret. But you were always a headstrong girl. Has this Jamie Brown ever told you who or what his parents were, or where he comes from? I don't ask about his forbear, for he does not look like a lad who has ever had ancestors; and you a Frazer of Lovat! Fie, for shame, Margaret ! Who is this Jamie Brown?"

"He is James Brown, Doctor of Medicine of the University of Edinburgh: a good, clever young man, whom I love with my whole heart," replied Margaret, reddening.

"Hoot! is that the way for a maiden to speak? Where does he come from? Who are his kinsfolk? Unless he can give a pretty good account of his family and prospects, I shall just bid him begone, Margaret; and that I tell you fairly."

"Uncle" (her eyes were filling with hot indignant tears), "I am of age; you know he is good and clever; else why have you had him so often to your house? I marry him, and not his kinsfolk. He is an orphan. I doubt if he has any relations that he keeps up with. He has no brothers nor sisters. I don't care where he comes from."

"What was his father? " asked Professor Frazer coldly.

"I don't know. Why should I go prying into every particular of his family, and asking who his father was, and what was the maiden name of his mother, and when his grandmother was married?"

"Yet I think I have heard less Margaret Frazer speak up pretty strongly in favour of a long line of unspotted ancestry."

"I had forgotten our own, I suppose, when I spoke so. Simon, Lord Lovat, is a creditable great-uncle to the Frazers! If all tales be true, he ought to have been hanged for a felon, instead of beheaded like a loyal gentleman."

"Oh! if you're determined to foul your own nest, I have done. Let James Brown come in; I will make him my bow, and thank him for condescending to marry a Frazer."

"Uncle," said Margaret, now fairly crying, "don't let us part in anger! We love each other in our hearts. You have been good to me, and so has my aunt. But I have given my word to Doctor Brown, and I must keep it. I should love him, if he was the son of a ploughman. We don't expect to be rich; but he has a few hundreds to start with, and I have my own hundred a year"

"Well, well, child, don't cry! You have settled it all for yourself, it seems; so I wash my hands of it. I shake off all responsibility. You will tell your aunt what arrangements you make with Doctor Brown about your marriage; and I will do what you wish in the matter. But don't send the young man in to me to ask my consent! I neither give it nor withhold it. It would have been different, if it had been Sir Alexander."

"Oh! Uncle Frazer, don't speak so. See Doctor Brown, and at any rate, for my sake, tell him you consent! Let me belong to you that much! It seems so desolate at such a time to have to dispose of myself, as if nobody owned or cared for me."

The door was thrown open, and Doctor James Brown was announced. Margaret hastened away; and, before he was aware, the Professor had given a sort of consent, without asking a question of the happy young man; who hurried away to seek his betrothed, leaving her uncle muttering to himself.

Both Doctor and Mrs. Frazer were so strongly opposed to Margaret's engagement, in reality, that they could not help showing it by manner and implication; although they had the grace to keep silent. But Margaret felt even more keenly than her lover that he was not welcome in the house. Her pleasure in seeing him was destroyed by her sense of the coldness with which he was received, and she willingly yielded to his desire of a short engagement; which was contrary to their original plan of waiting until he should be settled in practice in London, and should see his way clear to such an income as would render their marriage a prudent step. Doctor and Mrs. Frazer neither objected nor approved. Margaret would rather have had the most vehement opposition than this icy coldness. But it made her turn with redoubled affection to her warm-hearted and sympathising lover. Not that she had ever discussed her uncle and aunt's behaviour with him. As long as he was apparently unaware of it, she would not awaken him to a sense of it. Besides, they had stood to her so long in the relation of parents, that she felt she had no right to bring in a stranger to sit in judgment upon them.

So it was rather with a heavy heart that she arranged their future *menage* with Doctor Brown, unable to profit by her aunt's experience and wisdom. But Margaret herself was a prudent and sensible girl. Although accustomed to a degree of comfort in her uncle's house that almost amounted to luxury, she could resolutely dispense with it, when occasion required. When Doctor Brown started for London, to seek and prepare their new home, she enjoined him not to make any but the most necessary preparations for her reception. She would herself superintend all that was wanting when she came. He had some old furniture, stored up in a warehouse, which had been his mother's. He proposed selling it, and buying new in its place. Margaret persuaded him not to do this, but to make it go as far as it could. The household of the newly-married couple was to consist of a Scotchwoman long connected with the Frazer family, who was to be the sole female servant, and of a man whom Doctor Brown picked up in London, soon after he had fixed on a house a man named Crawford, who had lived for many years with a gentleman now gone abroad, who gave him the most excellent character, in reply to Doctor Brown's inquiries. This gentleman had employed Crawford in a number of ways; so that in fact he was a kind of Jack-of-all-trades; and Doctor Brown, in every letter to Margaret, had some new accomplishment of his servant's to relate. This he did with the more fulness and zest, because Margaret had slightly questioned the wisdom of starting in life with a man-servant, but had yielded to Doctor Brown's arguments on the necessity of keeping up a respectable appearance, making a decent show, &c., to any one who might be inclined to consult him, but be daunted by the appearance of old Christie out of the kitchen, and unwilling to leave a message with one who spoke such unintelligible English. Crawford was so good a carpenter that he could put up shelves, adjust faulty hinges, mend looks, and even went the length of constructing a box of some old boards that had once formed a packing-case. Crawford, one day, when his master was too busy to go out for his dinner, improvised an omelette as good as any Doctor Brown had ever tasted in Paris, when he was studying there. In short, Crawford was a kind of Admirable Crichton in his way, and Margaret was quite convinced that Doctor Brown was right in his decision that they must have a man-servant; even before she was respectfully greeted by Crawford, as he opened the door to the newly-married couple, when they came to their new home after their short wedding tour.

Doctor Brown was rather afraid lest Margaret should think the house bare and cheerless in its half-furnished state; for he had obeyed her injunctions and bought as little furniture as might be, in addition to the few things he had inherited from his mother. His consulting-room (how grand it sounded!) was completely arranged, ready for stray patients; and it was well calculated to make a good impression on them. There was a Turkey-carpet on the floor, that had been his mother's, and was just sufficiently worn to give it the air of respectability which handsome pieces of furniture have when they look as if they had not just been purchased for the occasion, but am in some degree hereditary. The same appearance pervaded the room: the library-table (bought second-hand, it must be confessed), the bureau, that had been his mother's, the leather chairs (as hereditary as the library-table), the shelves Crawford had put up for Doctor Brown's medical books, a good engraving on the walls, gave altogether so pleasant an aspect to the apartment that both Doctor and Mrs. Brown thought, for that evening at any rate, that poverty was just as comfortable a thing as riches. Crawford had ventured to take the liberty of placing a few flowers about the room, as his humble way of welcoming his mistress, late autumn-flowers, blending the idea of summer with that of winter, suggested by the bright little fire in the grate. Christie sent up delicious scones for tea; and Mrs. Frazer had made up for her want of geniality, as well as she could, by a store of marmalade and mutton hams. Doctor Brown could not be easy in his comfort, until he had shown Margaret, almost with a groan, how many rooms were as yet unfurnished, how much remained to be done. But she laughed at his alarm lest she should be disappointed in her new home; declared that she should like nothing better than planning and contriving; that, what with her own talent for upholstery and Crawford's for joinery, the rooms would be furnished as if by magic, and no bills, the usual consequences of comfort, be forthcoming. But, with the morning and daylight, Doctor Brown's anxiety returned. He saw and felt every crack in the ceiling, every spot on the paper, not for, himself, but for Margaret. He was constantly in his own mind, as it seemed, comparing the home he had brought her to with the one she had left. He seemed constantly afraid lest she had repented, or would repent having married him. This morbid restlessness was the only drawback to their great happiness; and, to do away with it, Margaret was led into expenses much beyond her original intention. She bought this article in preference to that, because her husband, if he went shopping with her, seemed so miserable if he suspected that she denied herself the slightest wish on the score of economy. She learnt to avoid taking him out with her, when she went to make her purchases; as it was a very simple thing to her to choose the least expensive thing, even though it were the ugliest, when she was by herself, but not a simple painless thing to harden her heart to his look of mortification, when she quietly said to the shopman that she could not afford this or that. On coming out of a shop after one of these occasions, he had said -

"Oh, Margaret, I ought not to have married you. You must forgive me, I have so loved you."

"Forgive you, James?" said she. "For making me so happy? What should make you think I care so much for rep in preference to moreen? Don't speak so again, please!"

"Oh, Margaret! but don't forget how I ask you to forgive me."

Crawford was everything that he had promised to be, and more than could be desired. He was Margaret's right hand in all her little household plans, in a way which irritated Christie not a little. This feud between Christie and Crawford was indeed the greatest discomfort in the household. Crawford was silently triumphant in his superior knowledge of London, in her favour upstairs, in this power of assisting his mistress, and in the consequent privilege of being frequently consulted. Christie was for ever regretting Scotland, and hinting at Margaret's neglect of one who had followed her fortunes into a strange country, to make a favourite of a stranger, and one who was none so good as he ought to be, as she would sometimes affirm. But, as she never brought any proof of her vague accusations, Margaret did not choose to question her, but set them down to a jealousy of her fellow-servant, which the mistress did all in her power to heal. On the whole, however, the four people forming this family lived together in tolerable harmony. Doctor Brown was more than satisfied with his house, his servants, his professional prospects, and most of all with his little energetic wife. Margaret, from time to time, was taken aback by certain moods of her husband's; but the tendency of these moods was not to weaken her affection, rather to call out a feeling of pity for what appeared to her morbid sufferings and suspicions, a pity ready to be turned into sympathy, as soon as she could discover any definite cause for his occasional depression of spirits. Christie did not pretend to like Crawford; but, as Margaret quietly declined to listen to her grumblings and discontent on this head, and as Crawford himself was almost painfully solicitous to gain the good opinion of the old Scotch woman, there was no rupture between them. On the whole, the popular, successful Doctor Brown was apparently the most anxious person in his family. There could be no great cause for this as regarded his money affairs. By one of those lucky accidents which sometimes lift a man up out of his struggles, and carry him on to smooth, unencumbered ground, he made a great step in his professional progress; and their income from this source was likely to be fully as much as Margaret and he had ever anticipated in their most sanguine moments, with the likelihood, too, of steady increase, as the years went on.

I must explain myself more fully on this head.

Margaret herself had rather more than a hundred a year; sometimes, indeed, her dividends had amounted to a hundred and thirty or forty pounds; but on that she dared not rely. Doctor Brown had seventeen hundred remaining of the three thousand left him by his mother; and out of this he had to pay for some of the furniture, the bills for which had not been sent in at the time, in spite of all Margaret's entreaties that such might be the case. They came in about a week before the time when the events I am going to narrate took place. Of course they amounted to more than even the prudent Margaret had expected; and she was a little dispirited to find how much money it would take to liquidate them. But, curiously and contradictorily enough, as she had often noticed before, any real cause for anxiety or disappointment did not seem to affect her husband's cheerfulness. He laughed at her dismay over her accounts, jingled the proceeds of that day's work in his pockets, counted it out to her, and calculated the year's probable income from that day's gains. Margaret took the guineas, and carried them upstairs to her own*secretaire* in silence; having learnt the difficult art of trying to swallow down her household cares in the presence of her husband. When she came back, she was cheerful, if grave. He had taken up the bills in her absence, and had been adding them together.

"Two hundred and thirty-six pounds," he said, putting the accounts away, to clear the table for tea, as Crawford brought in the things. "Why, I don't call that much. I believe I reckoned on their coming to a great deal more. I'll go into the City to-morrow, and sell out some shares, and set your little heart at ease. Now don't go and put a spoonful less tea in to-night to help to pay these bills. Earning is better than saving, and I am earning at a famous rate. Give me good tea, Maggie, for I have done a good day's work."

They were sitting in the doctor's consulting-room, for the better economy of fire. To add to Margaret's discomfort, the chimney smoked this evening. She had held her tongue from any repining words; for she remembered the old proverb about a smoky chimney and a scolding wife; but she was more irritated by the puffs of smoke coming over her pretty white work than she cared to show; and it wan in a sharper tone than usual that she spoke, in bidding Crawford take care and have the chimney swept. The next morning all had cleared brightly off. Her husband had convinced her that their money matters were going on well; the fire burned briskly at breakfast time; and the unwonted sun shone in at the windows. Margaret was surprised, when Crawford told her that he had not been able to meet with a chimney-sweeper that morning; but that he had tried to arrange the coals in the grate, so that, for this one morning at least, his mistress should not be annoyed, and, by the next, he would take care to secure a sweep. Margaret thanked him, and acquiesced in all plans about giving a general cleaning to the room; the more readily, because she felt that she had spoken sharply the night before. She decided to go and pay all her bills, and make some distant calls on the next morning; and her husband promised to go into the City and provide her with the money.

This he did. He showed her the notes that evening, locked them up for the night in his bureau; and, lo, in the morning they were gone! They had breakfasted in the back parlour, or half-furnished dining-room. A charwoman was in the front room, cleaning after the sweeps. Doctor Brown went to his bureau, singing an old Scotch tune as he left the dining-room. It was so long before he came back, that Margaret went to look for him. He was sitting in the chair nearest to the bureau, leaning his head upon it, in an attitude of the deepest despondency. He did not seem to hear Margaret's step, as she made her way among rolled-up carpets and chairs piled on each other. She had to touch him on the shoulder before she could rouse him.

"James, James!" she said in alarm.

He looked up at her almost as if he did not know her.

"Oh, Margaret!" he said, and took hold of her hands, and hid his face in her neck.

"Dearest love, what is it?" she asked, thinking he was suddenly taken ill.

"Some one has been to my bureau since last night," he groaned, without either looking up or moving.

"And taken the money," said Margaret, in an instant understanding how it stood. It was a great blow; a great loss, far greater than the few extra pounds by which the bills had exceeded her calculations: yet it seemed as if she could bear it better. "Oh dear!" she said, "that is bad; but after all - Do you know," she said, trying to raise his face, so that she might look into it, and give him the encouragement of her honest loving eyes, "at first I thought you were deadly ill, and all sorts of dreadful possibilities rushed through my mind, it is such a relief, to find that it is only money"

"Only money!" he echoed sadly, avoiding her look, as if he could not bear to show her how much he felt it.

"And after all," she said with spirit, "it can't be gone far. Only last night, it was here. The chimney-sweeps - we must send Crawford for the police directly. You did not take the numbers of the notes?" ringing the bell as she spoke.

"No; they were only to be in our possession one night," he said.

"No, to be sure not."

The charwoman now appeared at the door with her pail of hot water. Margaret looked into her face, as if to read guilt or innocence. She was a *protegee* of Christie's, who was not apt to accord her favour easily, or without good grounds; an honest, decent widow, with a large family to maintain by her labour, that was the character in which Margaret had engaged her; and she looked it. Grimy in her dress, because she could not spare the money or time to be clean, her skin looked healthy and cared for; she had a straightforward, business-like appearance about her, and seemed in no ways daunted nor surprised to see Doctor and Mrs. Brown standing in the middle of the room, in displeased perplexity and distress. She went about her business without taking any particular notice of them. Margaret's suspicions settled down yet more distinctly upon the chimney-sweeper; but he could not have gone far; the notes could hardly have got into circulation. Such a sum could not have been spent by such a man in so short a time; and the restoration of the money was her first, her only object. She had scarcely a thought for subsequent duties, such as prosecution of the offender, and the like consequences of crime. While her whole energies were bent on the speedy recovery of the money, and she was rapidly going over the necessary steps to be taken, her husband "sat all poured out into his chair," as the Germans say; no force in him to keep his limbs in any attitude requiring the slightest exertion; his face sunk, miserable, and with that foreshadowing of the lines of age which sudden distress is apt to call out on the youngest and smoothest faces.

"What can Crawford be about?" said Margaret, pulling the bell again with vehemence. "Oh, Crawford!" as the man at that instant appeared at the door.

"Is anything the matter?" he said, interrupting her, as if alarmed into an unusual discomposure by her violent ringing. "I had just gone round the corner with the letter master gave me last night for the post; and, when I came back Christie told me you had rung for me, ma'am. I beg your pardon, but I have hurried so," and, indeed, his breath did come quickly, and his face was full of penitent anxiety.

"Oh, Crawford! I am afraid the sweep has got into your master's bureau, and taken all the money he put there last night. It is gone, at any rate. Did you ever leave him in the room alone?"

"I can't say, ma'am; perhaps I did. Yes; I believe I did. I remember now, I had my work to do; and I thought the charwoman was come, and I went to my pantry; and sometime after Christie came to me, complaining that Mrs. Roberts was so late; and then I knew that he must have been alone in the room. But, clear me, ma'am, who would have thought there had been so much wickedness in him?"

"How was it that he got into the bureau?" said Margaret, turning to her husband. "Was the lock broken?"

He roused himself up, like one who wakens from sleep.

"Yes! No! I suppose I had turned the key without looking it last night. The bureau was closed, not locked, when I went to it this morning, and the bolt was shot." He relapsed into inactive, thoughtful silence.

"At any rate, it is no use losing time in wondering now. Go, Crawford, as fast as you can, for a policeman. You know the name of the chimney-sweeper, of course," she added, as Crawford was preparing to leave the room.

"Indeed, ma'am, I'm very sorry, but I just agreed with the first who was passing along the street. If I could have known"

But Margaret had turned away with an impatient gesture of despair. Crawford went, without another word, to seek a policeman.

In vain did his wife try and persuade Doctor Brown to taste any breakfast; a cup of tea was all he would try to swallow; and that was taken in hasty gulps, to clear his dry throat, as he heard Crawford's voice talking to the policeman whom he was ushering in.

The policeman heard all and said little. Then the inspector came. Doctor Brown seemed to leave all the talking to Crawford, who apparently liked nothing better. Margaret was infinitely distressed and dismayed by the effect the robbery seemed to have had on her husband's energies. The probable loss of such a sum was bad enough; but there was something so weak and poor in character in letting it affect him so strongly as to deaden all energy and destroy all hopeful spring, that, although Margaret did not dare to define her feeling, nor the cause of it, to herself she had the fact before her perpetually, that, if she were to judge of her husband from this morning only, she must learn to rely on herself alone in all cases of emergency. The inspector repeatedly turned from Crawford to Doctor and Mrs. Brown for answers to his inquiries. It was Margaret who replied, with terse, short sentences, very different from Crawford's long, involved explanations.

At length the inspector asked to speak to her alone. She followed him into the room, past the affronted Crawford and her despondent husband. The inspector gave one sharp look at the charwoman, who was going on with her scouring with stolid indifference, turned her out, and then asked Margaret where Crawford came from -- how long he had lived with them, and various other questions, all showing the direction his suspicions had taken. This shocked Margaret extremely; but she quickly answered every inquiry, and, at the end, watched the inspector's face closely, and waited for the avowal of the suspicion.

He led the way back to the other room without a word, however. Crawford had left, and Doctor Brown was trying to read the morning's letters (which had just been delivered); but his hands shook so much that he could not see a line.

"Doctor Brown," said the inspector, "I have little doubt that your man-servant has committed this robbery. I judge so from his whole manner; and from his anxiety to tell the story, and his way of trying to throw suspicion on the chimney-sweeper, neither whose name nor whose dwelling he can give; at least he says not. Your wife tells us he has already been out of the house this morning, even before he went to summon a policeman; so there is little doubt that he has found means for concealing or disposing of the notes; and you say you do not know the numbers. However, that can probably be ascertained."

At this moment Christie knocked at the door, and, in a state of great agitation, demanded to speak to Margaret. She brought up an additional store of suspicious circumstances, none of them much in themselves, but all tending to criminate her fellow-servant. She had expected to find herself blamed for starting the idea of Crawford's guilt, and was rather surprised to find herself listened to with attention by the inspector. This led her to tell many other little things, all bearing against Crawford, which a dread of being thought jealous and quarrelsome had led her to conceal before from her master and mistress. At the end of her story the inspector said -

"There can be no doubt of the course to be taken. You, sir, must give your man-servant in charge. He will be taken before the sitting magistrate directly; and there is already evidence enough to make him be remanded for a week, during which time we may trace the notes, and complete the chain."

"Must I prosecute?" said Doctor Brown, almost lividly pale. "It is, I own, a serious loss of money to me; but there will be the further expenses of the prosecution, the loss of time, the...."

He stopped. He saw his wife's indignant eyes fixed upon him, and shrank from their look of unconscious reproach.

"Yes, inspector," he said; "I give him in charge. Do what you will. Do what is right. Of course I take the consequences. We take the consequences. Don't we, Margaret?" He spoke in a kind of wild, low voice, of which Margaret thought it best to take no notice.

"Tell us exactly what to do," she said very coldly and quietly, addressing herself to the policeman.

He gave her the necessary directions as to their attending at the police-office, and bringing Christie as a witness, and then went away to take measures for securing Crawford.

Margaret was surprised to find how little hurry or violence needed to be used in Crawford's arrest. She had expected to hear sounds of commotion in the house, if indeed Crawford himself had not taken the alarm and escaped. But, when she had suggested the latter apprehension to the inspector, he smiled, and told her that, when he had first heard of the charge from the policeman on the beat, he had stationed a detective officer within sight of the house, to watch all ingress or egress; so that Crawford's whereabouts would soon have been discovered, if he had attempted to escape.

Margaret's attention was now directed to her husband. He was making hurried preparations for setting off on his round of visits, and evidently did not wish to have any conversation with her on the subject of the morning's event. He promised to be back by eleven o'clock; before which time, the inspector assured them, their presence would not be needed. Once or twice, Doctor Brown said, as if to himself, "It is a miserable business." Indeed, Margaret felt it to be so; and, now that the necessity for immediate speech and action was over, she began to fancy that she must be very hard-hearted, very deficient in common feeling; inasmuch as she had not suffered like her husband, at the discovery that the servant, whom they had been learning to consider as a friend, and to look upon as having their interests so warmly at heart was, in all probability, a treacherous thief. She remembered all his pretty marks of attention to her, from the day when he had welcomed her arrival at her new home by his humble present of flowers, until only the day before, when, seeing her fatigued, he had, unasked, made her a cup of coffee, coffee such as none but he could make. How often had he thought of warm dry clothes for her husband; how wakeful had he been at nights; how diligent in the mornings! It was no wonder that her husband felt this discovery of domestic treason acutely. It was she who was hard and selfish, thinking more of the recovery of the money than of the terrible disappointment in character, if the charge against Crawford were true.

At eleven o'clock her husband returned with a cab. Christie had thought the occasion of appearing at a police-office worthy of her Sunday clothes, and was as smart as her possessions could make her. But Margaret and her husband looked as pale and sorrow-stricken as if they had been the accused, and not the accusers.

Doctor Brown shrank from meeting Crawford's eye, as the one took his place in the witness-box, the other in the dock. Yet Crawford was trying, Margaret was sure of this, to catch his master's attention. Failing that, he looked at Margaret with an expression she could not fathom. Indeed, the whole character of his face was changed. Instead of the calm, smooth look of attentive obedience, he had assumed an insolent, threatening expression of defiance; smiling occasionally in a most unpleasant manner, as Doctor Brown spoke of the bureau and its contents. He was remanded for a week; but, the evidence as yet being far from conclusive, bail for his appearance was taken. This bail was offered by his brother, a respectable tradesman, well known in his neighbourhood, and to whom Crawford had sent on his arrest.

So Crawford was at large again, much to Christie's dismay; who took off her Sunday clothes, on her return home, with a heavy heart, hoping, rather than trusting, that they should not all be murdered in their beds before the week was out. It must be confessed, Margaret herself was not entirely free from fears of Crawford's vengeance; his eyes had looked so maliciously and vindictively at her and at her husband as they gave their evidence.

But his absence in the household gave Margaret enough to do to prevent her dwelling on foolish fears. His being away made a terrible blank in their daily comfort, which neither Margaret nor Christie, exert themselves as they would, could fill up; and it was the more necessary that all should go on smoothly, as Doctor Brown's nerves had received such a shook at the discovery of the guilt of his favourite, trusted servant, that Margaret was led at times to apprehend a serious illness. He would pace about the room at night, when he thought she was asleep, moaning to himself and in the morning he would require the utmost persuasion to induce him to go out and see his patients. He was worse than ever, after consulting the lawyer whom he had employed to conduct the prosecution. There was, as Margaret was brought unwillingly to perceive, some mystery in the case; for he eagerly took his letters from the post, going to the door as soon as he heard the knock, and concealing their directions from her. As the week passed away, his nervous misery still increased.

One evening, the candles were not lighted, he was sitting over the fire in a listless attitude, resting his head on his hand, and that supported on his knee, Margaret determined to try an experiment; to see if she could not probe, and find out the nature of the sore that he hid with such constant care. She took a stool and sat down at his feet, taking his hand in hers.

"Listen, dearest James, to an old story I once heard. It may interest you. There were two orphans, boy and girl in their hearts, though they were a young man and young woman in years. They were not brother and sister, and by-and-by they fell in love; just in the same fond silly way you and I did, you remember. Well, the girl was amongst her own people; but the boy was far away from his, if indeed he had any alive. But the girl loved him so dearly for himself, that sometimes she thought she was glad that he had no one to care for him but just her alone. Her friends did not like him as much as she did; for, perhaps, they were wise, grave, cold people, and she, I dare say, was very foolish. And they did not like her marrying the boy; which was just stupidity in them, for they had not a word to say against him. But, about a week before the marriage-day was fixed, they thought they had found out something, my darling love, don't take away your hand, don't tremble so, only just listen! Her aunt came to her and said: 'Child, you must give up your lover: his father was tempted, and sinned; and, if he is now alive, he is a transported convict. The marriage cannot take place.' But the girl stood up and said: 'If he has known this great sorrow and shame, he needs my love all the more. I will not leave him, nor forsake him, but love him all the better. And I charge you, aunt, as you hope to receive a blessing for doing as you would be done by, that you tell no one!' I really think that girl awed her aunt, in some strange way, into secrecy. But, when she was left alone, she cried long and sadly to think what a shadow rested on the heart she loved so dearly; and she meant to strive to lighten his life, and to conceal for ever that she had heard of its burden; but now she thinks "Oh, my husband! how you must have suffered" as he bent down his head on her shoulder and cried terrible man's tears.

"God be thanked!" he said at length. "You know all, and you do not shrink from me. Oh, what a miserable, deceitful coward I have been! Suffered! Yes - suffered enough to drive me mad; and, if I had but been brave, I might have been spared all this long twelve months of agony. But it is right I should have been punished. And you knew it even before we were married, when you might have been drawn back!"

"I could not; you would not have broken off your engagement with me, would you, under the like circumstances, if our cases had been reversed?"

"I do not know. Perhaps I might; for I am not so brave, so good, so strong as you, my Margaret. How could I be? Let me tell you more. We wandered about, my mother and I, thankful that our name was such a common one, but shrinking from every allusion in a way which no one can understand, who has not been conscious of an inward sore. Living in an assize town was torture; a commercial one was nearly as bad. My father was the son of a dignified clergyman, well known to his brethren: a cathedral town was to be avoided, because there the circumstance of the Dean of Saint Botolph's son having been transported was sure to be known. I had to be educated; therefore we had to live in a town; for my mother could not bear to part from me, and I was sent to a day-school. We were very poor for our station no! we had no station; we were the wife and child of a convict, poor for my mother's early habits, I should have said. But, when I was about fourteen, my father died in his exile, leaving, as convicts in those days sometimes did, a large fortune. It all came to us. My mother shut herself up, and cried and prayed for a whole day. Then she called me in, and took me into her counsel. We solemnly pledged ourselves to give the money to some charity, as soon as I was legally of age. Till then the interest was laid by, every penny of it; though sometimes we were in sore distress for money, my education cost so much. But how could we tell in what way the money had been accumulated?" Here he dropped his voice. "Soon after I was one-and-twenty, the papers rang with admiration of the unknown munificent donor of certain sums. I loathed their praises. I shrank from all recollection of my father. I remembered him dimly, but always as angry and violent with my mother. My poor, gentle mother! Margaret, she loved my father; and, for her sake, I have tried, since her death, to feel kindly towards his memory. Soon after my mother's death, I came to know you, my jewel, my treasure!"

After a while, he began again. "But, oh, Margaret! even now you do not know the worst. After my mother's death, I found a bundle of law papers, of newspaper reports about my father's trial. Poor soul! why she had kept them, I cannot say. They were covered over with notes in her handwriting; and, for that reason, I kept them. It was so touching to read her record of the days spent by her in her solitary innocence, while he was embroiling himself deeper and deeper in crime. I kept this bundle (as I thought so safely!) in a secret drawer of my bureau; but that wretch Crawford has got hold of it. I missed the papers that very morning. The loss of them was infinitely worse than the loss of the money; and now Crawford threatens to bring out the one terrible fact, in open court, if he can; and his lawyer may do it, I believe. At any rate, to have it blazoned out to the world, I who have spent my life in fearing this hour! But most of all for you, Margaret! Still, if only it could be avoided! Who will employ the son of Brown, the noted forger? I shall lose all my practice. Men will look askance at me as I enter their doors. They will drive me into crime. I sometimes fear that crime is hereditary! Oh, Margaret! what am I to do?"

"What can you do?" she asked.

"I can refuse to prosecute."

"Let Crawford go free, you knowing him to be guilty?

"I know him to be guilty."

"Then, simply, you cannot do this thing. You let loose a criminal upon the public."

"But, if I do not, we shall come to shame and poverty. It is for you I mind it, not for myself. I ought never to have married."

"Listen to me. I don't care for poverty; and, as to shame, I should feel it twenty times more grievously, if you and I consented to screen the guilty, from any fear or for any selfish motives of our own. I don't pretend that I shall not feel it, when first the truth is known. But my shame will turn into pride, as I watch you live it down. You have been rendered morbid, dear husband, by having something all your life to conceal. Let the world know the truth, and say the worst. You will go forth a free, honest, honourable man, able to do your future work without fear."

"That scoundrel Crawford has sent for an answer to his impudent note," said Christie, putting in her head at the door.

"Stay! May *I* write it?" said Margaret.

She wrote: -

"Whatever you may do or say, there is but one course open to us. No threats can deter your master from doing his duty.

"Margaret Brown."

"There!" she said, passing it to her husband; "he will see that I know all; and I suspect he has reckoned something on your tenderness for me."

Margaret's note only enraged, it did not daunt, Crawford. Before a week was out, every one who cared knew that Doctor Brown, the rising young physician, was son of the notorious Brown, the forger. All the consequences took place which he had anticipated. Crawford had to suffer a severe sentence; and Doctor Brown and his wife had to leave their house and go to a smaller one; they had to pinch and to screw, aided in all most zealously by the faithful Christie. But Doctor Brown was lighter-hearted than he had ever been before in his conscious lifetime. His foot was now firmly planted on the ground, and every step he rose was a sure gain. People did say that Margaret had been seen, in those worst times, on her hands and knees cleaning her own door-step. But I don't believe it, for Christie would never have let her do that. And, as far as my own evidence goes, I can only say that, the last time I was in London, I saw a brass-plate, with "Doctor James Brown" upon it, on the door of a handsome house in a handsome square. And as I looked, I saw a brougham drive up to the door, and a lady get out, and go into that house, who was certainly the Margaret Frazer of old days, graver; more portly; more stern, I had almost said. But, as I watched and thought, I saw her come to the dining-room window with a baby in her arms, and her whole face melted into a smile of infinite sweetness.

3010588R00054

Printed in Great Britain
by Amazon.co.uk, Ltd.,
Marston Gate.